Contents

short stories by

BERLIE
DOHERTY

winner of the Carnegie Medal

Running on Ice

mammoth

First published in Great Britain in 1997 by Mammoth
an imprint of Reed International Books Ltd
Michelin House, 81 Fulham Road, London SW3 6RB
and Auckland and Melbourne

This collection copyright © 1997 Berlie Doherty
Owls are Night Birds © Berlie Doherty 1989
originally broadcast on BBC Radio 4 Morning Story
first published in *Streets Ahead*, Methuen Children's Books, 1989
Ghost Galleon © Berlie Doherty 1985
originally broadcast on BBC Radio 4 Schools
first published in *Cold Feet: An Anthology of Horror Stories*, Hodder & Stoughton Children's
Books, 1985
Shrove Tuesday © Berlie Doherty 1992
first published in *Mother's Day*, Methuen Children's Books, 1992
Casting Off © Berlie Doherty 1996
first published in *Women and Home*, 1996 as *Mam's Day Out*
Summer of Ladybirds © Berlie Doherty 1987
first published in *Summer of Ladybirds*, Methuen Children's Books, 1987
Sweet Caroline © Berlie Doherty 1996
first published in *Heart to Heart*, Mammoth, 1996
Hurry Please © Berlie Doherty 1994
first published in *Ghostly Haunts*, Pavilion Books Ltd, 1994
Nightmare, © Berlie Doherty 1987
first published in *Beware, beware*, Hamish Hamilton Children's Books, 1987

The moral rights of the author and cover illustrator have been asserted

ISBN 0 7497 2873 6

A CIP catalogue record for this title is available from the British Library

Typeset by Avon Dataset Ltd, Bidford on Avon, B50 4JH
Printed in Great Britain by Cox & Wyman Ltd, Reading, Berkshire

CONTENTS

CONTENTS

For Miriam Hodgson
who loves short stories

1 Owls Are Night Birds

Elaine was always a little in front of Steven as they scrambled up the slope. It was so steep that they had to heave themselves up by clinging on to the coarse sprouting grass. When Elaine hauled herself up at last on to the top path she stood watching Steven, not helping him, as loose stones scuttled under his feet.

'Hot!' she gasped. 'Too hot!'

The path was dusty and rutted. It would lead them through the donkey field, past the new housing estate and the infant school, and on up the hill to their home.

'Come on, Steven.' Elaine set off again as soon as her brother had pulled himself over the tip of the slope. For a moment he lay on the grass at the side of the path, listening to the thud of her feet. Far away he could hear the drone of the city, like a hushed roar. The sound never stopped, day and night. It was the sound of foundries, hammering like a heart. It was the sound of cars and lorries and buses, always on the move, like blood pumping through veins. It was the sound of half a million people breathing.

He felt as if he was drowning in the stale air of the city's breath. 'I'm a lizard,' he thought. 'I'll dry up here in the sun; then she'll be sorry.' He stood up and ran along after her, stooping to search through the dense foliage for bilberries. He found some that the birds had left, and crouched down so he could cram them into his mouth. 'They're saving my life,' he thought. 'She'll die.'

'I'm sick of you,' his sister shouted, impatient. 'Come on. I'll buy you some lemonade at Mr Dyson's, if you hurry.'

'Race you to the donkey field!' he yelled, and she took up his challenge and broke into a loose run as the path flattened and swung into the shelter of overhanging trees. He stumbled after her, his shoes slapping the hard earth, watching the swing of her yellow hair. 'Can't make it. I'm a dead man.' He nursed a stitch that bent him sideways. He watched Elaine as she clambered up the leaning stone wall that surrounded the donkey field. She held herself there, motionless, with her hand lifted to shield her eyes. He limped up to her, drawing in his breath and groaning so that she wouldn't laugh at him for losing the race, but she swung her arm behind her in a warning gesture, and he pulled himself up beside her and sat with his legs straddling the hump of the wall; silent.

He saw immediately what she was looking at. A large white bird moved across the field towards them; a bird with a broad heavy head and wide blunt wings. It swung upwards, its great wings driving it like a swimmer through still water, and it drifted, bullet-headed, a huge silent moth, lifting itself soundlessly, while the air hung quiet around it. In the middle of the field the donkeys pressed and nudged each other, flicking their ears idly, unconscious of the dark shadow gliding over them.

'What is it?'

'It's an owl,' said Elaine softly. She couldn't take her eyes off it.

Steven slid off the wall and lay with the long grass criss-crossed over him. 'But owls are night birds.' He followed the slow flight of the bird quartering the field. With a last wide sweep that swung it high above their heads it left the field and floated across the wide valley, and was lost among the dark trees that shadowed the river on the far side; miles away.

Elaine slid down beside him and they trudged across the field. Steven pointed out some deep trenches that had been cut across the far end. They stretched out in a line from the end of the village lane to the beginning of the city houses, and they seemed to be huge squares dug into the soil. They walked slowly round them.

'What d'you think these are?' Steven asked. 'Why should someone dig up the donkey field?'

'I dunno,' said Elaine. 'Donkeys had better watch it, or they'll drop in.'

They both giggled.

'Come on,' said Steven. 'Let's ask Mr Dyson about that bird.'

He raced away from her, and she followed him slowly, her mind on the great white bird with sunlight like cream across its back.

Mr Dyson's corner shop was at the end of the lane that led up to their house. From there he'd sold sweets and drinks to generations of children on their way to and from school. You could hardly call it a shop now. At one time it had been crammed with ropes and buckets and bacon and socks and all the oddments that people in a village might want to buy in a hurry. But then, a few years ago, old Mr Dyson had had a stroke, and the village people had started going down to the supermarket that had opened up on the main road down to the city. Mr Dyson's stroke had left him partially paralysed. He never went out any more. His wife had kept the shop going so that at least he'd see the people who came in to buy, and they were mostly children, who knew that they could spend all the time in the world making their choices. She baked daily, and the warm sweet smell of new-baked bread and cakes snapped at you as you came up the hill, drawing you in. The shop part was really their front room, and at the jingle of the bell, old Mr Dyson would struggle out of the back room and greet the visitor with a shout of pleasure.

'I'll give you some money,' Elaine said. 'I'll wait out here.' Steven pulled her in. She was frightened of Mr Dyson now. His body was curiously twisted, so that one arm hung useless and one leg dragged to the side, and he walked with a laborious hopping rock-shuffle. His speech slurred one consonant into the other, making it impossible for anyone to understand him without watching his eyes, and Elaine was frightened of doing this. Usually she pushed her money across the counter to him and took her sweets and ran, letting the door jangle shut behind her and breathing in the outside air. But Steven loved him. He would climb on to the high stool that was put out for people who couldn't choose their sweets in a hurry and he and Mr Dyson would struggle to talk to each other. Sometimes, if they got stuck, Mrs Dyson would come out from the back and translate for them. She was sad and old and little, and hardly ever smiled.

Today Mr Dyson was dispirited. He leaned across the counter with his good arm, flapping his hand at the wasps that buzzed above the sticky cakes.

'Hey! Mr Dyson!' Steven shouted as he ran in.

The old man looked up, pleased. 'Hey! Hey!' he shouted back, and nodded to the cane stool. 'What have you two been up to today?' he seemed to say. You could just tell by the vowels.

'Mr Dyson! Wait till I tell you what we've seen!'

Elaine hung back. After the brilliance of the summer sunshine the shop was dark and gloomy. It was as if all that daylight no longer existed. She hated the dim stuffiness of the place. She watched the strip of yellow sticky paper that hung from the light bulb above the counter. It was stuck with the dead and dying bodies of wasps and flies and bluebottles, and it swivelled round slowly with the draught of air they'd brought in with them from outside. She longed to dive back out into the sunlight again.

'It was a bird, Mr Dyson, a great white one, like a ghost.'

'Like an owl,' said Elaine, cross.

'But it couldn't have been an owl, could it? They're night birds.'

Elaine wanted to tell him about the strange coldness it had put on them. Maybe that was what Steven had meant.

Mr Dyson frowned and nodded and called his wife in to help him out, and she came in with a jug of home-made lemonade that was all frothy and cloudy and swimming with pips, and poured some out for the two children.

'Come on Elaine,' she said, and Elaine edged forward and sat awkwardly on the other chair. The woman watched her husband as he talked, and spoke to him in the same sort of brief unfinished words. He seemed very tired, and kept shifting his position. The children drank, watching them.

'He reckons it's a barn owl,' Mrs Dyson said at last. 'An albino barn owl. A bit of a freak. That's why it's so white. And if its hearing and eyesight are weak, then it can't hunt by night, so it has to come out by day when seeing's easier. Fancy, he says, by all them new houses.'

Mr Dyson muttered something again and she translated it, but Steven beat her to it with a laugh of triumph.

'He says we're a pair of lucky jiggers to see it, an' all.'

Mr Dyson shook his head and swung his heavy body round, as if he were tired of this conversation, and heaved himself into the back room. His wife took the glasses from the children and put them on her tray.

'When he was a young man,' she told them quietly, 'he liked nothing better than to be up walking in the hills. You could walk for miles in them days, either direction, and still be in the country. And birds was his hobby, watching birds all hours, when he was young, and well.'

'We saw something else as well,' Steven said. 'Big holes. In the field.'

Mrs Dyson shook her head at him and looked quickly towards the back room, as if making sure that her husband hadn't heard. Then she took the tray into the back without saying goodbye, and Steven and Elaine left their money on the counter and went outside, squeezing past the door so they didn't make the shop bell jangle.

A few days later Elaine and Steven went back to the donkey

field, and there was the barn owl again.

'Barney!' Steven whispered, watching it.

They both felt the same thrill of excitement and strange surge of uneasiness as the air became silent and the bird moved strongly and soundlessly round them, and at last drifted away to its home.

'Tell him! I'm going to tell him!' Steven shouted. His heart was thudding with excitement as he raced out of the field to Mr Dyson's shop. Elaine trailed after him, and stopped to look at the holes in the earth. They were deeper now. They were proper trenches, roped off in big squares. A huge yellow fork-lift truck was parked by the gate, and beyond it, a workmen's portacabin. She walked down past the end hole square. After that was the new road. She could see nothing but houses from there, spreading down the long hill in a pattern of pink and grey roofs, down, down, to the far throbbing valley that was the heart of the city.

'Hey!' Mr Dyson laughed as Steven burst into the shop.

'Hey!' said Steven. 'We've seen it again!'

Mr Dyson chuckled as he listened to Steven, indicating that he wanted him to crawl under the counter flap and to come through with him to the back of the cottage. Mrs Dyson was baking. The room was neat and small, and as dark as the shop. Mr Dyson knelt down on one knee with his bad leg stretched behind him and searched through a pile of oddments under the table. At last he fished out what he was looking for. It was a large book.

'*Bird Journal*,' Steven read. 'Is this from when you were young and well, Mr Dyson?'

Mrs Dyson swung round to chastise him, but the old man chuckled and fingered through the carefully hand-written pages with their listings and sketches of birds he'd observed. He folded the book back on its first clean page.

'Pen, love,' he sounded to his wife, and she, floury and smiling now, found him one.

'Barn owl', he wrote.

'Barney,' Steven told him, and Mr Dyson wrote it in brackets next to the heading. 'Sighted, 3 p.m. Friday, August 3rd and Tuesday, August 7th. The donkey field.'

Mrs Dyson found some pencils and Steven sketched the owl in flight, and when he left Mr Dyson was sitting at the kitchen table, his tongue pressed out between his teeth like a child's, shading in Steven's sketch with coloured pencils.

Elaine was waiting for Steven outside the shop. 'They're building,' she told him.

'Building?' he repeated, puzzled.

'In the donkey field. They're building something there.'

'They can't,' he said flatly. 'It's the last bit of country left before the city. They can't build there.'

'Anyway,' he thought. 'It belongs to Barney now, that field.'

From then on the donkey field was Steven's favourite haunt. Elaine went with him a couple of times but by the time she'd seen Barney twice more she was bored. At least, that's what she told Steven. She loved to watch the owl's slow flight, but she hated the drone of the trucks and building lorries down at the bottom of the field, and the loud shouts of the workmen. She hated what she was seeing, as the earth holes were filled in with cement and tons of red bricks were tipped out nearby.

And she dreaded the visits to Mr Dyson's afterwards. The dimness and the stuffiness of the shop closed round her like winter nights, chasing away the summer. She felt strangely as if the donkey field and Barney were things they'd made up for the old man's benefit. For the first time ever, Steven and Elaine started to drift apart. They didn't even realise it was happening.

'Coming to the donkey field?' Steven asked her one day. She shrugged and followed him slowly out of the house, and then just didn't bother to go down the road after him, and he didn't bother to go back for her. She watched him running off down the hill and couldn't explain the sadness she felt inside herself. She rang up a school friend and arranged to meet her in town, and they spent that day and most of the rest of the holiday touring the boutiques and trying on new clothes. She wanted to look like the city girls, who always looked fresh and bright. She was sick of the country clothes she wore at home, all faded cottons and old jeans. They made her look too young.

'Guess what my brother's doing now?' she said to her friend Anna, one day. 'He's lying in a donkey field.'

'What for?' Anna asked, astonished.

'Watching a silly old owl!'

The two girls exploded into giggles, and turned themselves round in front of the shop mirror, admiring themselves in the dresses they couldn't afford to buy.

Mr Dyson loved Steven's visits. He wrote up his journal every day. Once Steven found an owl pellet near the trees and carried it, warm in his hand to the old man; a trophy, to the dark room where Mr Dyson had imprisoned himself. They rolled it open and sketched the tiny mouse bones they found in it. Mr Dyson had long forgotten the misery and resentment he'd felt when he first heard about Barney. The pellet was his find now, just as much as it was Steven's.

Sometimes Mrs Dyson would stand at the doorway of the shop watching out for Steven. 'Come on, love! He's waiting!' she'd sing out, and she'd leave the shop door propped open to let in the daylight. She brought flowers into the house and bustled round them while they talked, or sat, listening peacefully to their strange and awkward conversations. For the first time in years she forgot to be worried about her husband. She coaxed him into their little back garden where he could sit out and watch the cloud patterns on the far hills, and read the bird books Steven brought him from the library. And whenever Steven came there was always a glass of golden ginger beer or pale lemonade or apple juice for him, and new scones spread with home-made jam with strawberries whole and plump in it.

Sometimes they heard trucks trundling past on their way to the field. They seemed to make the whole cottage shake. Mr Dyson would look at his wife, worried and questioning, and she would look at Steven, willing him to keep his mouth shut. Steven always stopped to look at the buildings as he came past. The squares of bricks were as high as his waist now, and there was a gap in the front and the back of every one of them, just wide enough for someone to go in and out.

And then Barney left the field. Day after day Steven ran down there and lay in the long grass scanning the sky. He would race down on his way to the big shops on the estate, or first thing in the morning, or early evening, and the donkeys would always trot over and nuzzle him. But he hadn't come for the donkeys, or for the looping swallows. He was convinced that the albino owl had died. One day the donkeys were gone from the field too, and another row of trenches had been dug. He ran down to the first lot of buildings. The lines of bricks were higher. Rectangular spaces were left on all the sides. The holes that were big enough to walk in and out of were covered over at the top, and he knew for the first time what he had known in his heart for weeks. 'Doors!' he said out loud. 'Houses! They've joined us up with the city.'

He picked up a handful of rubble and started chucking it through the doorway and window holes, enjoying the thud of it as it spattered against the inside walls.

'Oi!' One of the builders yelled at him. 'What you up to? Eh?'

'You've killed Barney!' Steven shouted. 'This is his hunting field. You've killed him!'

The man shouted at him to clear off, and Steven ran home, straight past Mr Dyson's shop, not even looking. For the next few days he kept going down to the field, just in case, and he came slowly past the shop. Sometimes he just tapped on the window and shook his head.

He spent all Saturday in the field when the workmen were not working. He wandered miserably round the buildings, wondering if he could get the cement mixer to work, thinking about filling in all the door and window holes, and he knew that it was useless. The city had come to the village, and there was no stopping it. He heard a great roar surge up from somewhere far below, and he ran to the edge of the field, listening. It was the sound of a football match. It was a goal. He heard the excited chanting of the crowd and found his own voice in it, 'Ci-ty! Ci-ty! Ci-ty!' he murmured, and then louder and louder, yelling it out, a thrill of excitement inside him. 'CI-TY!'

And that was the last day of the summer holidays. He and Elaine started back at school the next week. They never sat together on the bus any more. She had her own friends now.

Mr Dyson sat all day at his table, waiting for the boy to come. He listened inside himself for Steven's animated chatter that had brought so much of the summer sunshine into his dark home. His house had grown gloomy and quiet again. He was lost for things to do, and Mrs Dyson became anxious and unsmiling again, watching him. He kept his journal open and ready on the table, and at the end of the day he would write with his good hand, 'No Barney today.'

'No Steven today,' Mrs Dyson would say, looking over his shoulder. That was what he meant.

When the letter came from the council telling them that the cottages in their lane were to be demolished to make way for the new development she hid it in fear from him. She spent hours in her garden, pulling up weeds uselessly. 'It's coming, it's coming,' she said to herself. 'There's no stopping cities.' They'd have a modern house with proper facilities. They'd be surrounded. It would make a change. It would break the old man's heart.

The last day in September was brilliantly sunny. Steven and Elaine had nothing to do, and decided to go down to the river together. Steven was shy about asking Elaine to come with him now. They picnicked there and she lay back, catching a last suntan, while Steven skimmed pebbles on the water and watched the wagtails and dippers bobbing on the stony banks. They'd come the long way because that would bring them back on their favourite walk past the farm with the goats and eventually, up the long hill to the donkey field. They didn't mention Barney to each other. He belonged to a part of the summer that was past.

'Race you to the donkey field!' he challenged as they panted up the slope.

'Not a donkey field now!' she reminded him. 'Housing estate.'

They scrambled up the last steep slope and Elaine swung along the path, with Steven close behind her, and as they clambered up the stone wall there it was again; the white owl, in the full brilliance of the late afternoon: Barney. Low over the grass, and below them, with its broad strong head and its pale soft back, quartering the field of half-grown houses with slow lifts of its wings. There was no other movement in the field. Not a sound.

Elaine and Steven stood, breathless, on the wall, following Barney's route across the field, and suddenly Steven's eyes were stopped by an unfamiliar bundle in the grass, a twist of drab colour, humped at an angle. He turned sharply to Elaine and she smiled and nodded and laid her hand on his arm. Mr Dyson, lying in the long grass at the side of the field, raised his arm slowly as if in a salute, and rested his hand as a shield above his eyes, watching the movements of the daylight owl.

Steven thought of the old man dragging himself to the front of his shop; his slow unsteady shuffle. It must have taken him hours to get himself down the lane, past the little school, through all the rubble of the building site and across the rough grass to where he lay now, folded in a corner of the field. He forgot to watch Barney, and when he looked again the bird was making its last circle of the field. It rose higher and higher, right into the line of the sun, nearly blinding him, and then it drifted out across the valley to its dark shelter. Steven knew that he would never see it again.

The voice of the city surged up like a throaty roar and died away again. Steven plunged across the grass to the old man.

'What d'you think of Barney, Mr Dyson? I told you, didn't I?'

Mr Dyson lay with his hand still resting across his eyes, like a small child suddenly fallen asleep. The boy stood back a little, and his sister joined him. Together they looked down at the old man, with the grass criss-crossed against his face, and the small bees droning round him, and the sun warm on him.

Elaine put her arm round Steven's shoulder.

'We'd better go,' she told him. 'We'd better tell her.'

'But, he isn't asleep, is he?' said Steven doubtfully, staring down at the old man, at the humped twist of his body and the strange expression of peace on his face.

'No. He isn't asleep. He's all right.'

And the brother and sister walked slowly from their summer field in silence together.

2 Ghost Galleon

My home is on farmland, in the flat fens of East Anglia. They say that many years ago my fields were sea, and that tides rose and fell over the fields that sway with wheat and in the groves that are now tight with trees. I discovered this when I was twelve years old and staying for a time in this very house which now belongs to me, but which at that time belonged to my grandfather. It was in that same year that I discovered that my name, Charles Oliver, is not English but Spanish: Carlos Olivarez. But the story of how I came to have this name, and how I learnt the truth of it, is almost beyond belief.

It happened soon after I came to the house. I had asked my grandfather if the Oliver family had always lived in that part of the country. Grandad didn't answer me at first; he seemed to be weighing the question up. And then he said: 'If you're asking that, then I think it's time I moved you up to the little bedroom at the front of the house. Just for a bit.'

He had that way about him, that made him seem full of unfathomable secrets – people say I have that way with me, too. Anyway, I didn't ask him anything more, and he didn't tell me, but that night my sleeping things were moved right up to the top floor of the house into the little bedroom that my Grandad said he had slept in when he was a boy. There was nothing special about this room. It was smaller than the one I was used to, and I didn't like it much. It smelt damp, and it was dark and dusty. I had the feeling that no-one had slept in it for years – maybe not since Grandad was my age – sixty years back! The window looked out on to a grove of beech trees, and beyond that, miles and miles of fields, and the long, dark horizon of the east.

It was because it faced east that I woke up so early the next morning, with the first streak of dawn pushing itself like needles into my eyes. It must have been about four o'clock. I couldn't get back to sleep again, and I lay in bed looking at the way the strange light cast reflections like ripples on my wall and ceiling. I remember thinking that it must be because of the angle of the light coming up through the moving branches of the trees. And the trees sounded different, too, this side of the house. I could hear the wind sighing through them, and it was a comforting sort of sound to lie in bed and listen to, even at that unearthly hour.

It was a regular, gentle, rushing sound, with a to and fro heave to it; a rhythm. A kind of breathing; like the sea.

It *was* the sea!

I jumped out of bed and ran to the window. There was hardly any light to see by, still, only that first pale streak where the sun would soon be, but the gleam of it stretched a sort of path over something that was dark and moving, rolling, slow and steady, and wave on wave of it, with here and there ghostly flecks of white. My sense told me that it was the wind moving across the fields of wheat, but my heart thudded in my throat with excitement and fear and told me that it was the sea! Yet the trees were there, black, between me and the skyline, and all I could make out was by peering through their silhouetted branches, and all I could hear of the waves was through the creaking of their tall trunks. And suddenly I realised that one of those trunks – no, two, three – three of the trunks were moving. They came gliding behind the pattern of the trees, and were just visible over the tops, and as they passed behind a clearing my racing heart stopped, because what I could see now wasn't trees moving, with looped branches all at angles. Clear as anything, for that second when my heart stood still, I know I saw the masts and riggings of a sailing ship.

Even then I didn't realise how massive a ship it was till it came properly into view; then I could see that it had many decks, so the whole thing towered out of the water like a huge floating castle; and that it had three or four masts, each with its own cross-spars and sails. I saw it in silhouette, blacker than a shadow against the light, but so clear that all the tight ropes of its rigging traced a pattern like lace from spar to spar; like a cradle of fine web. And yet it was enormous. I'd seen pictures of ships like that. It was a ship of war of four hundred years ago.

It was a galleon.

I raced down the stairs and out of the house with my pyjama jacket flapping open and all the dogs of the farm yapping after me. I ran till I came to the very edge of the grove, and fell back with weariness against one of the trunks, sliding my back down it till I was crouched on the ground. The sun was flooding up now, pushing up into the sky as if it owned the world, glaring out across not sea, but fields, as I'd always known, and the trees round me stood still and silent with not even a breath of wind to stir them. My thudding steps had sent rabbits scudding across the grass, white tails bobbing like flashes of light. When I could breathe steadily I stood up again and looked across the flat plains. A harsh cry, like a sob, caught my attention, and I saw a great grey-white bird lift its heavy wings and drift slowly out across the line of the sun, and away out of sight.

'Heron!' I shouted after it in disappointment, and back came its strange, sad cry.

*

At breakfast I played safe.

'Grandad. I had a funny dream last night.'

'Did you, Charlie?' he said. 'What was it about?'

'I dreamt that the fields behind the trees were the sea.'

'Did you now?' said Grandad. 'Well, that wasn't such a funny dream. A long time ago, hundreds of years ago, most of this land *was* sea. All this farmland was reclaimed from the sea. If this house had been here then the waves would have come lapping over the doorstep. And I should think whoever lived here would have been a fisherman, instead of a farmer.'

I buttered my toast carefully. Had I known that already? I was sure I hadn't. But *had* I dreamt it?

I decided to pretend I wasn't much interested in the answer to my next question, in case it sounded silly.

'Would there have been galleons?' I asked carelessly.

'Oh yes. It's said, Charlie, that this coast was the route of the Spanish Armada, in 1588. They came right up here and over the top of Scotland.' Long after my Grandad had left the table I was still sitting there, still smoothing and smoothing a skin of butter over my cold toast, till Gran took it away from me and reminded me gently that there were farm jobs to be done, and that my help was needed.

So I kept my secret to myself. That night I couldn't wait to get back up to my little room at the top of the house. I pushed up the window and leaned out. I could see the line of familiar trees, dark and quiet in the twilight. I pulled my chair over and sat there, my chin propped on my hands, staring out as the gloom gathered the sky into its darkness till there was nothing more to see, and nothing to hear in all that sleeping farmland.

I didn't know I'd gone to sleep till I was pulled awake by what seemed to be a cry coming out of the darkness. I leaned out of the window to listen again but this time I caught that surge and sigh that I'd heard the night before – the wind in fields of wheat; or the waves of the sea, rolling. It was too dark even to see the trees. A gust of air brought in a cool dampness and, what's more, there was a tang to it, sharp and unmistakable with salt on its breath, and I knew what that was all right. It was the smell the wind brought with it when the tide was coming in.

And then, it seemed, I heard the cry again.

Again I raced down the stairs. I thudded down the track to where I knew the trees would be, even though there was no shape of them to go by. But light was beginning to come up, just a glow that was pale gold, and I knew then with a rush of fear that there *were* no trees, and that the cold sting on my cheeks was the fling of spray. I turned to look back, and saw that the big old farmhouse building was gone, and that all that was left was the low shape of a cottage or hut, no bigger than one of our barns. But there wasn't time even to think about that. Water was lapping round my bare feet. I heard a massive creaking, and could just make out the shape of an enormous bulk moving somewhere far out in front of me, with little lights swinging on it, and the bark of voices coming from it, and into the line of the day's first light came gliding first the prow, then the hull, masts and all, and riggings, and straining sails, of a galleon.

For a moment the sun burst up. I saw the silk banners streaming scarlet and silver and gold, and the white sails arched back like wings in flight, and the lettering picked out in gold: *La Garza*. Spanish. Then a cloud dulled the sunlight and all I could make out were the poop lanterns gleaming like animal eyes, and the dark shape of it gliding quiet as death over the fields of my grandad's farm.

There was the cry again. This time I knew even before the light came up again what it was. A child was in the water, and he was shouting for help.

I was a good swimmer, so my next action was completely instinctive. I never even stopped to think about the weirdness of the situation but waded out at once into the sea of four hundred years ago, up to my knees, up to my thighs, and then I plunged myself in and swam out in the direction of the dark bobbing head.

'*¡Ay! ¡Socorro!*' the voice cried. I'd no idea then what the words meant, but they'll stay in my memory for the rest of my life. It's Spanish. 'Help', it means.

'*¡Socorro!*'

There were times when I thought I'd never reach him. I kept losing sight of the bobbing head. Gulls' cries drowned his voice. The sea seemed to want to drag me down. But at last I did reach him, and he seemed to be half-dead by then. He had almost lost consciousness. I managed to hold him up somehow with my arm hooked under his armpit while I struggled to pull off my pyjama top. I'd been told at school how to make a kind of balloon out of it, but I never thought the day would come when I'd have to, or be able to. I kept going under with him, and the sea choked every breath I took. But at last I'd done it, and with both my arms round the boy I held on to the float and paddled for shore. I'd never swum so far before. I wanted to give up the battle and just leave go of him and let myself drift away and sleep. My body touched land at last, but I wasn't yet out of the sea. We were shored on a sandbank a few yards from the beach. Waves kept pulling me back, and I hadn't the strength to pull myself any further.

And I wouldn't have made those last few yards if a woman hadn't come running out of that little thatched cottage I'd seen earlier. She screamed something to me and waded in to the sea with her long skirts billowing round her. She caught us both by our armpits and dragged us out of the water, and dumped us like big gasping fish on dry land. 'Mercy on us, lad, what's this ye've caught?' she said in the strange accent of long ago. 'Tha's fished up some sort o' monkey!'

I rolled over on to my back and lay gaping up at her till her shape swam into focus and I had the strength to pull myself into a sitting position. She knelt by the boy, marvelling at his olive skin, his black hair and lashes, his spoiled velvet clothes.

'He's Spanish!' I panted. 'Can you help him?'

'Help a Spaniard!' She spat into the sand. She folded her arms and rocked her head sideways as though she couldn't make me out, either.

'Tha's asking me to help the enemy, son!'

I crawled over to the boy and lifted his head up. He coughed, and water streamed from his mouth like vomit.

'¡Ay!' he said weakly, lying back again.

'What a poor wretch he is!' The woman knelt by him and wrapped her shawl round his shivering body.

'You're all right!' I said to him. 'Don't worry. You'll be all right now.'

He opened his eyes at last. He looked terrified.

'You're in England!' I said. 'I'm Charlie. You?'

'Leave him be!' the woman said. 'He'll not understand thy talk!'

His eyes flitted from me to the woman and back again. He shook his head.

I pointed first to myself, then to him. 'Charles Oliver. You?'

'¿Yo? Carlos Olivarez. Charl Olibber.'

'Charles Oliver. Carlos Olivarez.'

'*Lo mismo.*'

'The same,' I said, and we stared as though we had always known each other.

The woman had moved away from us and was standing shielding her eyes against the early rising sun and looking out to sea. 'Methinks the boy will not return to Spain,' she said. 'See how his ship flies home!' Far away on the horizon now, right into the sunlight, the galleon scudded in full sail with all her banners streaming.

The boy Carlos pulled himself up with a terrible cry of grief.

'*¡La Garza! ¡La Garza!*'

I turned my eyes away at last from the retreating ship. The boy was gone, and the woman with him, and the little fishing cottage she'd come running down from. I was standing on grass, in our field, with our farmhouse behind us, and the field sloped down to a grove of beech trees and beyond that, field after field stretched out to the horizon where the early sun blazed like gold and the great winged heron rose into its path with its sad and solitary cry.

In a daze I went back into the house. This time I knew I must tell Grandad everything. I waited downstairs for him, scared to go back to bed in case I fell asleep and came to think of all these strange things as a dream. But my pyjamas were wet, and my skin tasted salt, and I could still remember the weight of the drowning boy in my arms.

As soon as Grandad was awake I told him my story. He took it in his old quiet way, not surprised.

'Well, you've answered your question, Charlie,' he said. 'You asked me if our family had always lived here, and the answer is – yes. Since the time of the Spanish Armada. The first member of our family to live here was a Spaniard.'

'Carlos Olivarez,' I said.

'And now you know more than I ever knew,' Grandad went on. 'You know how he came here, and why he stayed.'

'He was a ship's boy off a Spanish galleon, and he fell overboard, and was rescued by an English boy and a fisherwoman.'

It was still too much to take in. I remembered the look on the woman's face, and the thought of how she'd pitied the enemy and taken him into her house. If she hadn't . . . if Carlos hadn't been rescued from the sea . . . he'd have died out there. And none of us would have been born. Not me, nor my dad, nor my grandad, nor any of the long line of boys stretching right back to the sixteenth century. The thought of it all made me dizzy.

'Grandad, did the same thing happen to you when you slept up in that room? Is that why you wanted me to sleep up there?'

He shook his head. 'I thought I heard the sea when I slept up there. It puzzled me, but I never saw it. Your dad heard it too, and as a child it frightened him. *My* father told me he saw the sea, and heard the creakings of an enormous ship of some sort. And we've all heard the same cry out there at dawn. I don't think anyone ever saw the ghost galleon before you did, Charlie. And I don't suppose anyone will, now. It won't come back.'

'Why not?' I asked. In spite of all the terrible happenings of the night before I felt that I wanted to see that beautiful ship again. I felt as if I belonged to it, and that the galleon belonged to me . . .

'Why should it?' Grandad said. 'The ghost boy has been rescued. No need now for the ghost galleon to come in search of him any more. Is there?'

I knew Grandad was right. 'I think I'll go down tomorrow morning, all the same,' I said. 'Just in case it's there.'

'You'll see something, but it won't be the galleon,' Grandad said. 'You'll see what I see every morning at dawn. I'll come with you, Charlie.'

Well, I did go down with him the next morning, and what I saw filled me with a strange sadness, as if I was remembering it from long ago. Till the end of my life the sight of it will fill me with the same grief. Grandad and I went down together to the grove, and watched the startled white of the rabbits scurrying over the fields to safety. I saw the distant fields of wheat surging gold, like the sea with sunlight on it. I heard the wind sighing in the branches of the trees around me, like the breathing of waves. And when the sun was up I heard that strange, sad, half-human cry. I saw the heron lift its great heavy wings and drift out slowly towards the line of the sun, and what I saw then wasn't a bird any longer. It was Carlos Olivarez' galleon, *La Garza*: The Heron. It was arching back its sails like huge white wings and it was flying home on the winds of time to Spain. Without him.

3 Shrove Tuesday

Jenny came into the kitchen and sat on a stool watching her mother. She was making a batter for pancakes, beating milk and eggs into flour till the mixture in the jug was thick and creamy. She put a saucer on the top to let it stand for half an hour.

'You'll have to help me, Jenny,' she said, 'if you want pancakes for tea. I've got to be out at half-past six for night school. They're a nuisance, pancakes.'

'No, they're not,' said Jenny. 'They're fantastic. I wish we could have them once a week instead of once a year.'

'This time next year,' her mother sighed, 'you won't be eating any at all because you'll be worrying about your figure.'

Jenny pulled a face. 'Not me! I'd rather have pancakes than a figure any day.'

'Wait and see,' her mother smiled. 'Do these for me, will you?' She rolled a couple of oranges and a lemon across the work surface, and Jenny caught them just before they dropped off the edge. She loved working in the kitchen with her mother, just as she loved helping her dad in his woodshed. It gave them a special time together, just two of them. She always felt closer to them at times like this.

She quartered the fruits and arranged them in alternate strips of orange and yellow around a plate, then put them on the table with a tin of syrup.

'And brown sugar,' her mother said over her shoulder. 'You know your dad likes brown sugar on his pancakes.'

'How can I possibly remember that when we only have them once a year?' Jenny dipped her finger in the brown sugar and licked it. 'Mum,' she said. 'I've got something to tell you.' She waited with her back to her mother, her eyes closed.

Her mother was making a salad for the first course. She piled some wet lettuce leaves into a clean teatowel and gathered it up, shaking out the moisture over the sink. Jenny could feel the fine, cold spray from where she was standing. She bit her lip, willing her mother to stop.

'Have you put the cutlery out, Jen?'

'Mum.' Jenny came right up to her at the sink. 'I've got a boyfriend.'

Her mother half smiled to herself. 'Oh, well, that's all right,' she said, not looking up at her. 'Just so long as you don't start inviting him for pancakes too.'

'He wants me to go to the pictures with him on Friday.'

Her mother stopped shaking the lettuce and turned round to look at her. She saw a girl who was just a little smaller than herself, who had black wispy hair that was tied back in elastic bands, whose ankle socks were rumpled.

'That's out of the question,' she told her quietly.

Jenny had known that her mother would say that. All the same, she couldn't help the give-away disappointed tears that blurted up in her eyes. 'Why is it? Why is it?' Her voice was a plaintive wail, a little girl's voice, and she couldn't help it. She tried to steady it.

'For goodness' sake, you should know better than to ask me, even. Yesterday you were crying your eyes out because Lorraine's guinea pig had died. Today you're crying because I won't let you go waltzing off to the pictures with every lad you meet.'

'It's not every lad I meet. It's Alex Hartley and he's in my class.'

'You're not old enough.'

'I'm fourteen.' Jenny blew her nose on some kitchen paper. 'All my friends have got boyfriends.'

'So that's it.' Her mother turned back to the chopping board. She felt through a bowl of tomatoes for the firmest ones and began to slice them. The seeds and the flesh oozed out. Jenny watched her. She felt as if she hated her.

'First it's horses,' her mother said, matching her words to the rhythm of her slicing. 'Then it's roller boots, then it's some kind of fancy blouse with lace all over it, and now, for goodness' sake, it's boyfriends. Everyone else has got one first. It's always the same with you, young lady. You've got to have what everyone else has got.'

'I didn't get a horse.'

If Jenny's mother heard her she ignored it. 'Get Will and your dad, will you? Let's get this stuff eaten or I'll never get out tonight.'

The tone of her voice told Jenny that that was the end of the matter. Even so, she couldn't resist her parting shot as she went out of the kitchen.

'I could have just pretended I was going with Lorraine. That's what she does, you know.'

Her mother put the bowl of salad on the table and went to wash her hands at the sink. She could see Jenny going across the yard to the wall and hoisting herself up on it to shout down the entry for Will to come in, and grazing her knees as she slid down it again.

'Wait till she opens the back gate instead of climbing the wall,' she said to herself. 'That's when she'll be old enough for boys.'

But, all the same, her heart went out to the girl, remembering herself at that age, and how she had longed to wear stockings instead of socks, and had stolen her own mother's lipstick to wear at a birthday party. She smiled to herself, and it was with a kind of nostalgia that she turned away. She looked round her neat kitchen, its surfaces wiped and gleaming, the jug of batter ready and waiting to be cooked for her family's tea because it was Pancake Tuesday. She didn't even like pancakes herself.

Jenny went into the shed to get her father. It smelt of sawdust and oil, and a bare light bulb swung from the ceiling. Her father was bending over a long hutch, planing the sides. He looked up sharply when she opened the door, then grinned and jerked his head to tell her to come in and close the door behind her.

'Tea's ready.'

'Aye. I'll not be long now.' He reached out for a sheet of sandpaper and folded it round a block of wood. Then he rubbed it along the edge of the hutch in a tender, careful motion. Yellow dust powdered his hands.

'Is it finished, Dad?' Jenny squatted down to watch him.

'It's looking grand, don't you reckon?' Her dad stepped back to show her how he'd fitted mesh across the door of the hutch, and where he'd put in hinges so it could swing backwards and forwards without catching. He bent down and felt round the inside of the hutch, frowning, seeking for splinters with his fingers. She could see how the brown muscles on his forearms bulged, and how the hairs were scattered with dust.

'I'll get the catch fastened on while she's out at class. Then it's done.'

'What d'you think she'll say?'

Her father shrugged. 'She'll say nowt. When that little rabbit's tucked inside it, she'll say nowt.' His voice was low and warm, and she remembered the late-night stories he used to whisper to her in the dark, when she and he were the only ones awake in the house.

'Has Will seen it?'

'Not unless he's spied through the cracks in the shed. Wouldn't put it past him, little devil.'

He stood up again and spat on his hands, rubbing them together to get rid of the sawdust powder.

'Not salad again, is it?'

'And pancakes.'

'Am I sick to death of salad! I'll sneak a bit into my pocket for the little rabbit's first tea, I reckon,' he chuckled. 'And I'll run up the road for some chips as soon as she's gone out.'

'Chips are bad for the heart,' Jenny reminded him. 'Anyway, you'll be able to fill up on pancakes.'

Her dad threw a blanket across the hutch and switched off the light before he opened the door. Jenny watched him ducking between the flapping teatowels on the line. It was already dark. She reached up to unpeg them and he stopped to help her.

'Dad. Does someone called Ed Hartley work on the buses with you?'

'Ed Hartley? Aye, he does. Why d'you ask?'

Jenny shrugged. 'I don't know. His Alex is in our class.' She shoved some pegs in her pockets. She couldn't help grinning at her dad.

'Oh aye! Alex Hartley, eh? Got his eye fixed on our Jen, has he?' Her dad chuckled and put his arm round her. 'Is that it?'

Jenny giggled.

'He'll have to come round and fight your dad for you, tell him. You're going to marry me, aren't you?'

Mrs Yates spent most of the meal standing by the cooker, making the pancakes. She listened to the family chattering at the table while the batter sizzled in the hot pan. Her mind was on the piece of work she was supposed to have completed for night school. When the batter was golden brown and loose enough to shake it in the pan she stepped away from the cooker.

'Watch!' she said. 'And keep your fingers crossed.'

Will and Jenny clapped as the pancake flipped round in mid-air and landed with a soft flop in the pan.

As she poured the next lot of batter in, Mrs Yates thought about her homework again, solving problems in her head. Perhaps she'd get a good mark this time.

Jenny and Will had four pancakes each. He ran straight out

afterwards to play with his friends till bedtime, and Mrs Yates ran for her bus. Jenny and her dad did the washing-up between them, and as soon as he had gone out to the shed she rang her friend Lorraine.

'What did she say?' Lorraine asked.

'She said I can't.' Disappointment sobbed up inside her again. 'I hate her.'

'She'll come round in the end. Just keep asking her,' Lorraine said.

'She's not like that. If she says no, she means it. Will's been asking her and asking her for a rabbit, and she just gets madder and madder at him. She won't listen, not if she doesn't want to.'

'I thought you said he was getting a rabbit tomorrow.'

'Yes, but she doesn't know. Dad's just going to sneak it into our shed for him.'

They both started giggling. 'Get him to sneak Alex Hartley in as well.'

'I'll get him to make a hutch for him and his bike!'

After the phone call Jenny went out to talk to her dad. A bunch of late snowdrops gleamed in the dark and she bent down and picked them. She arranged them in a bowl in the kitchen, a present for her mum.

At night school Mrs Yates was doing a maths test. She did maths on Tuesdays and English on Thursdays. With a bit of luck she'd be sitting her A levels in a year or two; maybe applying for a university course after that. She kept her dreams to herself, though. At coffee-break she went downstairs to the coffee-lounge with the others. She and one of the other women, Ann, had become good friends through these courses. They had a lot in common. She looked forward to talking to Ann as much as coming to the classes.

'What do I do this for, Ann?' she said, laughing for the first time that day. 'My brain feels like a piece of knitting that's just dropped off its needles!'

'It's all very well for those young ones,' Ann agreed, indicating a group of school-leavers who were coming to the class to re-sit their exams. 'I'm working in a shop all day, rushed off my feet, dash home to cook tea . . .'

'Pancakes, and I can't stand the things!'

'And then it's this place, and then homework before I get to bed. And my brain's fizzing like a wasp's nest all night and I can't get to sleep!'

'I know,' Mrs Yates sighed. 'But what would we be doing if we weren't here?'

'Watching telly,' her friend agreed. 'And that's enough to send anyone round the twist.'

Mrs Yates sipped at her coffee. 'I had a shock tonight,' she said. 'My daughter wants a boyfriend, and she's only fourteen.'

'You'll not stop her now,' Ann warned her. 'Not now she's

interested. It would be like trying to stop the tide coming in. And if you try to stop her, she'll only hate you for it. Don't you trust her?'

The class began to move out of the coffee-bar. Clutching her books to her, Mrs Yates followed them. 'She's only a child,' she said at last. 'She's my little girl.'

Mr Yates always picked his wife up after classes. They often went for a quick drink on the way home, sometimes with people from the class. Mr Yates would just sit and smile at them and let them get on with their talking. He'd rather be down at the busmen's club, any day. When they got home that night Will was waiting on the stairs for them.

'What on earth are you doing out of bed?' Mrs Yates gasped. Her mind flew back to her earlier conversation with Jenny. 'She's not sneaked out, has she?' She had a picture of Jenny standing in a shop doorway somewhere, kissing and cuddling with some spotty lad from school.

'She's been sick,' said Will. He hunched his pyjama trousers up till the waist elastic was over his shoulders.

'It's all those pancakes,' Mrs Yates said, relieved. 'I knew it would happen.'

Jenny groaned from upstairs.

'As if I haven't had enough for today,' Mrs Yates said.

Her husband scooped Will up over his shoulder and carried him upside-down and giggling to his bed.

'And you'll have him sick, too,' she called, 'if you don't watch it.'

She went into Jenny's room.

'Did you do it down the toilet?' she asked.

'Mum, I feel awful,' Jenny moaned.

'Maybe you'll think twice before you guzzle four pancakes next time,' her mother said. 'I'll fetch you some boiled water to sip.'

She bent down and covered Jenny up with her quilt.

'My tummy hurts,' Jenny groaned.

'It will do, if you've been sick. Lie still now.'

'You don't know how much it hurts,' Jenny gasped.

Mrs Yates turned away. She knew Jenny was playing for sympathy, trying to make her feel guilty. Well, it wouldn't work. She was too old now for that kind of behaviour. She went downstairs and boiled up some water. Her kitchen gleamed in the moonlight. The snowdrops trailed out of their bowl, dead already, their white tips brown. Mrs Yates scooped them up and pushed them into the kitchen bin, and washed the bowl. Then she took the drink upstairs. Jenny was lying with her knees hunched up, groaning softly.

'Come on, it's not that bad,' her mother said.

'It is,' Jenny said. 'It's terrible.'

Her mother opened the window. 'There, that'll cool you down.' She put her hand on her daughter's forehead.

'Don't go,' Jenny whispered.

Mrs Yates hesitated for a moment. She was tired. She had to

go to work in the morning. 'I'll leave the door open,' she promised. 'I'll hear you over the landing.'

She went into her own room. From there she could hear the shuddering sobs of someone beginning to cry. She's trying to make me feel guilty, she thought. I know her tricks. Her husband was asleep already, his spectacles looped over the alarm clock, ready for tomorrow to start.

Some time later Will crept into their room. He hated going into his parents' room at night. His mother snored loudly and levelly. Sometimes Will would hear his father shouting at her to shut up. Sometimes, he knew, his father would creep downstairs, spectacles and alarm clock in his hand, and stretch himself out on the settee in the front room.

Will waited for a pause in the snores. 'Jenny's been sick again,' he said. He held his pyjama trousers bunched up by the waist in both his hands, because the elastic had snapped. 'She says she's got a terrible pain,' he shouted at the top of his voice.

Both his parents sat up in bed. Jenny moaned into the darkness.

'Doctor,' Mr Yates said.

'Not at this time of night,' his wife said.

'That's what they're paid for, you silly ass,' Mr Yates shouted.

Will knew it was only because he was worried.

*

Jenny's pain kept slipping away from her like a shiny eel and twisting back inside her again. She heard the doctor coming, and felt herself being lumped about as she was carried downstairs. She gazed up at Dad, who looked strange without his spectacles, and at Will, who was in Dad's arms, and something like a tickle in her memory reminded her that something nice was going to happen to Will soon though she couldn't remember what it was. She saw the ambulance waiting outside with its blue flashing light, and then she was being bobbed along to it with her head looking up at the stars. She climbed out of another wave of pain and knew she was speeding along in the ambulance and that Mum was there. That was all right; Mum bending towards her and holding her hand; Mum's kind round face looking worried and scared.

When the ambulance stopped she felt herself being bumped about again and wheeled into a brightly lit building with a white ceiling. There were people peering over her, large kind faces. Someone peeled off her clothes and put her into a shift that felt like a cardboard cutout. Then the walls narrowed and the pain grew as sharp as icicles that glittered and dripped with hurt, and then Mum wasn't there any more.

She lay in a kind of drowsy darkness. Something was pulling her out of it. She felt very calm, as if she were lying on her back and floating along on a dark, smooth river. But she couldn't make out the sound that was pulling her out of the water, from far away and long ago it came, then nearer and newer, a grunting, wheezing kind of sound that rose and fell, rose and fell in a deep rhythm. At last she pulled herself away from the sound and knew what it was.

'Mum,' she whispered. She couldn't believe how tiny and far away her voice was. 'Mum. You're snoring.'

Her mother jerked awake, unsure herself of where she was. She gazed round, aware of a bed near her with tubes strung above it. Day was coming cold and grey through some white shutters across the wide windows. She was sitting on a hard chair beside a hospital bed. She stood up, aching and cold, and looked down at her daughter. Jenny was as white as a doll, calm and quiet and grave, her eyelids closing, her dark hair spread round her on the pillow. She looked like a little girl again. And she looked like a young woman, serene.

'You've had your appendix out, love,' Mrs Yates said.

Jenny nodded. 'I thought so,' she whispered. Her mouth was dry.

'It's all over. It's all behind you now.'

'I feel sleepy,' Jenny murmured.

'That's right, love. You sleep properly now the anaesthetic's worn off. It'll do you good.'

Mrs Yates patted her daughter's hand.

'You've been a brave girl,' she said.

Jenny smiled.

Mrs Yates looked round at the chair. She must have slept on it for hours, waiting for Jenny to come round. She was stiff and cold. She looked back at Jenny. She wanted to pick her up and rock her in her arms as if she was a little baby again. She wanted to say she was sorry, and she didn't know how.

Jenny opened her heavy eyelids. 'You go and get some sleep, Mum.' Her voice was slurred and soft, calm and full of comfort. 'I'm all right.' She drifted off before she'd finished the last sentence. Mrs Yates knew she was right. There was nothing she could do for her now. The nurses knew what to do. Sadly she picked up her bag, gave Jenny's sleeping face a kiss, and tiptoed out of the ward.

By the time she got home her husband was getting Will ready for school.

'I'll drop him off at school and nip down to the hospital,' he told her. 'You get some kip.'

'Mummy,' said Will. 'There's something better than magic for me in the shed. Daddy's going to show it to me at lunchtime.'

'Is there?' Mrs Yates looked down at her little boy. She felt as if she'd been away from home for ages. Her head was heavy with worry and weariness.

'Bed,' her husband told her, helping her off with her coat.

Mrs Yates had something to do first. She swallowed hard.

'I don't suppose Jenny mentioned a boy to you, did she?'

Her husband laughed. 'Alex Hartley. Think there's a romance budding there.'

Mrs Yates looked out of the window. The snowdrops by the shed were a smudge of brilliance, huddled away from the wind.

'I think I'll give Lorraine a ring before school,' she said. 'She might just like to bring that lad round to see Jenny at visiting time.'

She glanced at her husband, and at Will, clean and eager for school with his new box of colouring pencils clutched in his hand.

'It won't do any harm, will it?'

And her husband touched her hand and said, 'No, love. It won't.'

4 Casting Off

I went with Mam to Glasgow. I didn't want her to come.

I was full of myself that day. Well, I was about to leave home, wasn't I? It was my first big step. Freedom at last, after seventeen years. And Mam had to come along with me. But I didn't want to hurt her feelings, so I said nothing. If I passed my interview and got accepted at the university I'd be away for good. And Mam used to live there, you see. She left Glasgow when she was my age, and she was wanting to show it to me. I could understand that. But I wanted to discover it for myself.

On the journey she was very excited, while I was tense with nerves. She flirted with the guard even before we got on the train. She was determined to enjoy her day out. Our tickets had come out of her dole money. 'This is our holiday this year,' she told me, and

I think it was true. So there we were, set for a long train ride together, and Mam had her magazines and a bag full of sandwiches for the journey, and a bit of knitting to finish off. She was making me a cardigan to wear at university.

The compartment was full of people underlining things on file paper and tapping away on laptop computers.

'Things must be pretty grim 'way the trains these days,' Mam said, 'if they huf'te rent oot the carriages as offices.'

A man sitting opposite us smirked and fished a portable telephone out of his brief-case, and for the first two hours of the journey he had loud and important conversations with himself. Mam kept sighing and nudging me and in the end she just snatched the telephone out of his hand. That's what she's like.

'Gie ma ears peace,' she said.

And he did.

'Mam!' I whispered, but she just smiled at me and put on her headphones.

'That's better,' she said. 'I can hear ma music noo.'

Mam. Why does she always embarrass me? I stared out of the window at the little vanishing snatches of real life going on outside and wondered whether everyone had trouble with their mothers. But it wouldn't last much longer.

One thing was certain though. She was not setting foot over

the university threshold when I went for my interview. I made quite certain she understood that.

'I wouldna dream of it,' she told me. 'I'm gonnie paint the toon rid.'

Oh, Mam.

I must say her face was a picture when we got off at Central Station and walked out into Argyle Street. Will I feel as romantic as this about Rotherham when I've been gone for eighteen years? She tucked her arm into mine and pushed her way through the shoppers as if she had divine right of way, pointing out the shops that had closed down and the shops that were new and the ones that were exactly the same.

'See yon pub? That's where your da' asked me to marry him – the pig!' she laughed. I'd never seen my dad. He certainly never married my mam. 'We had a right old sing-song. And then we went ta the pally and on the way hame I puked – or wis it him? I can'y remember!'

I could hardly take in her prattle. I was getting more and more tense about my interview. It was all I could think about.

'I think I ought to go now, Mam,' I said at last. I had visions of her trailing after me into the university building, clinging on to my arm, coming into the interview room and telling them all how good I was at writing poems, how she got me to write the verses on all the family birthday cards. She probably had that tartan handbag of hers stuffed full of them. 'Leave me, Mam. Leave me alone.' That was what my head was screaming out at her. 'It's my life now.'

'Tell me where to meet up with you, and I'll go.'

'You'll never find your way aboot on your ain,' she said. Her eyes were roving like little cameras, snapping up pictures of people, shops, buses, lights; shuffling and storing everything she saw. It was as if she was hoping to see someone in particular in all that crowd. My dad, perhaps. The ghost of herself at seventeen years old.

'I've got a map,' I reminded her. 'I know exactly where I'm going. But it might take a couple of hours.'

We had stopped at a point where the street forked and led on to a market.

'Here we are, the Barras!' she laughed. 'Ma maw had a stall here. Jist oor there. A used ta help her oot. Best place. You'll be able to get all your messages when you're at the uni'. You'll no be able to get them any cheaper, that's for sure.'

Hawkers were standing round, blowing into their hands, stamping their feet up and down to keep their circulation going. Some of the stalls had transistor radios tuned in to a radio play about Robert Louis Stevenson. I wondered if I might mention this at my interview.

'Here, before you go, just try this against you.' Mam snatched at a cardigan hanging from a rail outside the stall that used to be her mam's. It was a maroon zip-up, not unlike the ones she used to knit for me when I was about ten.

'A love you in this colour,' she said.

The stall-holder hovered near, all headscarf and cigarette, fingering the material in the same loving way. 'Will you look at the price!' Her voice was deeper than a man's. 'It would be cheaper to buy three of these than to knit just one yesel'!'

'Mam, where'm I going to meet you?'

She was rummaging through the jumpers. 'A could do all ma Christmas shopping and keep it by.' She fished out a tinselly silvered top and held it against herself. She cocked back her head playfully, her eyes shining.

'Bonny,' the stall-holder crooned.

I shook my head. 'No,' I said. 'I'm going. Now. Where do you want to meet me?'

'The People's Palace. There's a good cafe there,' the stall-holder suggested, recognising my agitation. 'Just away over that waste ground. You canna miss it.'

'Will that do, Mam?'

She nodded, the shiny blousy affair tucked under her chin now, other jumpers looped over her arm on their hangers.

'Bye Mam,' I said, as she drifted away. She hadn't even wished me luck.

I think my interview went well, until I was asked about my recent reading. My mind went a total blank then. I had a pile of books by my bed and couldn't summon up the title of one of them. 'It was something by Robert Louis Stevenson,' I stammered. 'No, about him. His autobiography. I mean, biography. I always get them mixed up.' I gazed out of the window, at the way drops of rain hung and bulged. In another room somewhere an insistent telephone rang. My interviewer coughed and shuffled my papers.

'Why did you particularly want to come to Glasgow?' he asked me. That was the only time he actually looked at me, little round brown eyes that reminded me of the buttons on Mam's going-out dress, the one that's too tight by several pounds, as she always says. He lingered in his look, making me hot and confused. I was sure that had been one of the questions on my application form. I couldn't remember what I had written. I wondered whether this was a trick question, and whether I would lose my chance of a place if I gave the wrong answer.

'One of the reasons,' I said, playing for time and caution, 'is because my mother was here.'

'English?'

'Scottish. Oh, English? No. Music.' The lie tumbled out like the mess that's been shoved into an untidy cupboard. I didn't even know if there was a music school in Glasgow University. What could I tell him, as his eyes rounded and bulged and refused to let me go? Mam lived with seven brothers and sisters in a tenement block that had been pulled down years ago. Was that enough reason for wanting to read English at Glasgow University? His eyes never left mine. They had turned to liquid, were pouring themselves into my skull.

'Instrument?'

'She doesn't play... she's a singer.'

'Ah! Voice!' he sighed. His eyes grew solid again. He put out their light and turned back to the papers on his desk.

When I got back to Argyle Street it was growing dark. I hurried through the Barras Market, half-expecting Mam to be there still, clutching her bargains. I was late. I skidded across a muddy patch of rough ground and into the museum of the People's Palace, pushed my way past the paintings and maps and found the tea room. There was a wrestling match going on there. Men in kilts and reddened backs were throwing each other about, silent except for the slap of their feet on the floor and the occasional grunts they gave. They were cheered on by a gang of smart middle-aged women and little boys. It was like a dance. Every now and then an official in a very smart kilt would come and point at one of the men and the crowd would clap. There was no sign of Mam. She would have enjoyed it. 'I've seen better meat on the butcher's slab!' she would have whispered, really loud too. I bought myself a hot chocolate piled high with cream and sat down to wait for her.

I kept going over the interview in my head. I imagined Mam in the room with me, the shriek of outraged laughter she would have given when she heard my story about her music. I knew she wouldn't come to the People's Palace. Why should she? Why should she wait for me? Hadn't I cast her off at last, just as I'd wanted to?

The match finished. The bulky men bowed, their sweat sour and ripe. The smart women whipped open their handbags and brought out mirrors in their cupped hands, discreetly bobbing lipstick. Their teacups all had red bows on the rim. I thought of Mam in her brown padded anorak from Oxfam, and the shoes she never thought of cleaning. Mam with her hair frizzled with a perm that was growing out, black at the roots. She didn't come to museums, even if they were called people's palaces. I should have known that. She would be loaded up with pink see-through carrier bags bulging with bargains for next year's Christmas presents. Their straps would be cutting her fingers. She would stop and buy a carton of tea from a street stall rather than sit in a cafe. She liked it better that way. But she would have loved the wrestlers.

I walked back through the empty market to Argyle Street. Most of the shops were closing. I headed for Central Station. I felt lonely. I was worried about Mam. Would she remember to get off the train at Sheffield? I began to run. I pictured myself on the train, searching through the compartments for her.

There was a crowd gathered on the pavement outside the pub she had pointed out to me earlier. People were cheering, and I thought there was a fight going on, a street brawl. I started to cross the road and then I paused, drawn back to the crowd by something that reminded me of home, our kitchen even. I was aware now of loud music, a familiar tune, a brave, wonderful voice singing. I knew the tune. It was a country-and-western song, Mam's favourite. Someone behind me was saying, 'Look at her! She's grand, that lassie,' and I stood on tiptoe to peer between the heads. It was not a fight they were watching. The music was piped but the voice was live enough. The crowd parted a little in response to my pushing.

The pub had a karaoke sign flashing above the door and I suddenly knew what it was they were all looking at, who it was that had made a crowd of cold people stop still on a rainy night in Glasgow. There she was, turning slowly as she sang, a microphone in her hand, her other hand held out to acknowledge her audience. As she turned she was catching their eyes and smiling like any television star. Her head was tilted back a little, showing the neckline of a tinselly silver top under her brown anorak. My mam it was, and they were all cheering her, all these people. My beautiful mam.

5 Summer of Ladybirds

'Paul! Where are you going?'

'Out! Anywhere. Out.'

The long hot summer dragged on endlessly. The heat became intolerable. It was too much effort to walk about. People stayed indoors, drawing their curtains against the sunlight. Even the nights were pitilessly hot. It was impossible to sleep. In the daytime fractious children squabbled and cried, and parents scolded them, too irritable to give them any comfort.

Inland the parched earth cracked and shrank. Grass died. The soil lay like grey dust, and forests were ravaged by fire. Scorched hillsides smoked.

And on the coast a small strange invasion was preparing. It was a plague of ladybirds. They swarmed across the barren earth to the hot sands, and bred there in their millions, taking possession of the beaches like summer tourists. Children came outdoors to capture them in jam jars, and squelched them underfoot. They crawled in sluggish bundles on stones, on kerbs, on railings, clinging obsequiously to clothes and hair, clinging to shrinking skin. They blundered in waspish, unfamiliar flight, or lay like red gleaming pools on the roadside, shifting lazily. Motorists drove blind in blood-red cars. And on the sands they lay drowned, cast backwards and forwards like bright beads by the tides.

The summer had gone wrong. The heat was hideous.

Late one August evening, when a copper sun was low over the estuary, Paul came down to the sands. Some council workers were shovelling up ladybirds into huge bins on the prom. Paul leaned against the railings, watching them, flicking his hand across his face from time to time.

'Some holiday!' he thought. 'Some rotten holiday!' He had spent the last few weeks cooped up in the holiday flat with his parents until a small knot of fury built up inside him. He felt as if he hated them; everything they did irritated him, yet there was no escape –

too hot to walk across the sandstone hills, or to lie in the fields, or to bathe in the sea. The heat had exhausted his mother. She lay on the couch like some lumpish Eastern princess, fanning herself with last night's newspaper, puffing out her lips as if breathing was too much effort. Paul had tried to be nice to her – this evening he had made the meal, but she had chewed it as though she expected to find a ladybird in every mouthful, and pulled out pieces between her teeth to line the plate with, like a reproach.

'Can't eat, love,' she sighed. 'Just can't eat. Take it away.'

His father sat inside his pipe smoke, cracking his fingers and listening to the radio; all day long, news and interviews and current affairs, rapid insistent voices, on and on and on . . . and the stem of his pipe stabbing out of his smoke cloud – 'What d'you think of that, Paul? Eh? What d'you think of that?'

'I'm going!' Paul had shouted. 'Out!'

As soon as he got outside he felt better, though the heat of the evening was still oppressive. His head throbbed. He felt as if he wanted to pick up a stone and smash it through the window of the holiday flat, knock his father's pipe for six and send the radio chattering and whistling into pieces across the floor.

He started to run, fiercely brushing ladybirds off his hair, shaking them from his hand. They landed heavily from a drunken flight and occasionally they nipped, sharply and tinily. Paul tried to avoid the red clusters on the pavement as he ran, but once he was on the prom he found it was impossible to go down the steps on to the beach without treading on them. He closed his eyes, and felt the step slithering under his foot.

He walked quickly along the shoreline away from the houses and towards Red Rocks. He always loved it there. It was a tiny bay curving into tall slabs of red sandstone. When he came here as a little boy he used to leap off the rocks into the soft sand. It was always good to watch the sunset there, slipping down between Hilbre Island and the long arm of the Welsh hills. He walked there now out of habit, not really aware of where he was walking, only of the anger and frustration that was driving him away from the house.

'That's the last time I go away with them,' he said to himself. 'It's worse than being at home with them. No bike. No telly. No Griffo. Holiday! I'd rather be at school! I'd rather do maths all summer!'

He pulled himself up on to the rocks, stamping on the hard black bubbles of bladderwrack, trying to crack them. The stomp of his foot thudded as though the ground was hollow, but there was another, brisker sound; a snap with a kind of rhythm to it. He stopped and listened, trying to identify it. He crept forward and peered over the edge of the rock. Crouching about three metres below him, and bending forward away from him, was a small girl. Her elbows jerked with rapid movement. He moved crabwise and soundless along the rock edge, trying to fathom what she was doing. A small stone crumbled away from his foot and bounced down near to her, but she didn't look up. In front of her she had a small pile of sticks, branches, which she was breaking up into smaller pieces, lying them side by side like logs ready to be rolled down to a river. When she had a handful ready she swung round and laid them in a crisscross pattern over a hole in the rock, balancing them with care so they didn't roll forward and spoil the pattern. She turned again to the pile of sticks and began to break up another set, laying them on the crisscross pile.

Paul jumped down from his ledge, spraying up sand with his hands and feet as he landed on all fours next to her. The girl looked up at him for a moment, frowning. She wasn't a child. She had a small, round, squashed face, with close-set eyes. Her fine brown hair was cut like a child's, fringed and short. Her bare arms and legs were plump, and her fingers short and stubby. She was thickly freckled, and her lips were moist with saliva dribble.

'Hello,' Paul said. 'What are you doing?'

She stared at him warily, laying her hands over the stick pile. She reminded him of a cat caught with a bird. He walked away from her and she bent down again immediately to her twig-snapping. He sat in a curve of the rock where the sand was cool. He was watching the swifts darting, but he could see her.

After a time she stood up and shook bits of clinging twig from her skirt. She rubbed her hands together, satisfied with her work. Then she fumbled in her pockets and brought out a box of matches, which she sniffed and shook close to her ear. She struck a match and held it up to watch the blue flame spurt and dwindle. She struck again and bent down to drop the match into the middle of the little crisscross pyre she had built. There was a slow spiral of grey smoke, then the flame flared like a tongue, separate from the pile. The girl laughed and knelt down, her hands over it, her face close to it. She could feel the touch of the heat on her cheeks. She laughed, low and humming, not at all like a child's laugh. Paul watched her, curious.

With a sudden swift movement she reached behind her and dragged a red plastic bucket towards the fire, and tipped it with two hands. The flame hissed and sank. The red stream from the bucket became separate, like drops of blood.

Paul came slowly over to her, disbelieving.

'You're burning ladybirds!'

She bent down again and fed her fire from the waiting pile of twigs, and set to breaking up another pile. Her small arms worked rapidly and deftly, snapping the dry twigs to identical lengths, laying them together neatly, and her eyes never left the crackling fire. She fed it again and then ran across the sands to the slipway. Paul watched her scooping up ladybirds in handfuls and ladling them into her child's bucket. He crouched down and put twigs on the fire for her, to bring the blaze back up, while she watched him. Then she emptied the bucket gradually, tipping it in small jerks, so its live contents slithered like water to the fire, spat and sizzled.

Paul laughed with her. She rocked herself down on to her knees. The ladybirds glistened on the stone like red berries bursting. The smoke curled softly, shrouding them.

'What d'you do that for?' asked Paul. 'It's cruel, that.'

The girl didn't seem to notice him. She broke her sticks slowly, captured by the fire.

'I'll fetch wood for you,' Paul offered. 'But I'll not burn ladybirds.'

He wandered up to the low gorse hedge that separated the bay from the camp site. There was one caravan left in the field, and as he watched a woman came out of it, stooped under a line of limp washing that was tethered to a hawthorn, and crossed the field to the lane that led to the village. She left the door of the caravan wide open.

Paul gathered up some dead twigs and took them back to the fire. The girl ran to him with the bucket brimfull again.

'You need a bigger one,' Paul told her. 'A kitchen bucket. We've got one.'

She didn't answer. She tipped her bucket slowly, swirling it now to make the dull red stream spiral round and round into the snuffling fire.

'I'll have to go. Shall I fetch you one tomorrow?'

But she was watching her flames, bent forward, eager, with her hair swung forward across her eyes. He shrugged and walked away from her, turning back to watch her in the dimming light. The sun had dipped but the sky was vivid, rich blue streaked with red, with black swifts dark and screaming against it. The girl's skin, her hair and arms, gleamed as she bent and swayed, and he heard the crack like pistol shots of sharp twigs snapping as he walked out over the sands to his village.

After Paul had gone the girl, Ruth, sat for a while by her small fire while the sky grew dark and the evening tide spread out towards the bay. She waited till the cream of foam crept into the stones, making the ashes hiss, and then she drew away. The tide would come no further now. She found her pumps and picked her way over the rocks and into the caravan field where she and her mother lived. Her mother had just come in.

'I thought you'd be in bed, Ruth. Where've you been till this time?'

'On beach.'

'On the beach!' her mother repeated, disgusted. 'Look at you! Look at the state of you! Sandy knees! You're more like six than sixteen.'

Ruth helped herself to some bread and jam and swung herself up on her bunk. She kicked her pumps off and sand trickled out of them. Her toes gleamed with the yellow crystals.

'Look at you! Pumps full of sand! At your age!'

Ruth sucked an ooze of jam from a split in her bread. 'I met a boy, Mum.'

Her mother looked at her sharply. 'I don't want you messing round with boys. You're too stupid.'

'I didn't talk to him.'

'I should think not.'

'He talked to me though.'

Her mother sighed. 'Ignore him, Ruth. You're not the type to go with boys.' She started to undress herself, her shadow on the caravan ceiling lumpy and squat in the dull light of the Gaz lamp. 'Anyway, boys and men, they're all the same. Leave them alone, or make use of them.'

Ruth lay back on her bunk and smiled. When the camp site had been full she used to watch the boys and girls of her own age. She used to love to see them going around together. She'd see the girls in the washrooms fluffing out their hair and giggling about the boys they'd met. She'd see the boys waiting outside for them, showing off for them as soon as they came out. Where the friend-ships were special she'd see the hands linking or the boy slipping his arm round his girl's shoulder, and kissing her where her hair touched her cheek. And then Ruth used to slip into the washrooms when they were empty and smile at her reflection, sweep back her thin hair and let it swing forward again to kiss her cheeks.

'We're going to have to move on in a few days, Ruth. I've had enough.'

Ruth rolled herself away from her mother's shadow. She had been expecting this. 'Don't go, Mum. We like this place best.'

'Don't be silly. How can we stay here? Empty camp site. Everyone's gone!'

'They might come back.'

'There's been no takings at all this week. Who's going to pay our wages when there's been no takings? We can't live off sea air.'

'Please, Mum. Don't move again.'

Her mother sighed. She stooped down into her bunk and turned off the Gaz lamp. It was too hot to lie under the clothes.

'Don't you forget to wash yourself,' she told Ruth.

Ruth didn't answer. Now that she was in darkness she rolled herself right over so that her knees tucked up almost under her chin. She bit hard against the crooked knuckles of her fingers, her eyes pressed tight shut. Outside the caravan she could hear the light rustle of grasses as the night creatures moved about. She could hear the sea washing against the rocks, like the cool swish of silk. Her mother's breathing deepened and steadied.

Please stay please stay please stay.

Ruth and her mother had spent the last six years running away and hiding. Now night had come again Ruth clearly remembered, as if it was all happening again, the night sounds of the house she had lived in as a little girl: doors banging, her mother and father shouting to each other in tired, heavy voices, lights on, lights off, more shouting, banging, lights, into the night, into daylight. She had lain in bed then as tonight curled up away from it all, and frightened. She remembered vividly and with a start of terror how on a particular night her mother had run into her room and lifted her out of her bed as though she'd been a baby and had carried her downstairs and out into the rain to a waiting taxi; how her father had come running out after them, his face bending towards her on the other side of the window, how the picture of him had blurred yellow as the taxi moved away. She remembered his voice over the engine sound: Please stay.

The mother and girl had trailed from town to town finding lodgings where her mother could pick up jobs. Wherever they went it meant a change of school for Ruth; the new horrors of children shying away from her strangeness, or taunting her with it.

Twice, in the first two years, her father had found them. Ruth could remember running in from school to see him standing there, unexpected, in the kitchen or the hall, her forbidden and undisguised surge of pleasure at seeing him evaporating as her mother came between them.

'Come home!' her father had begged.

'Home!' her mother had hissed. 'This is my home. Home is where I live.'

After he had been they would always move again.

Then, last summer, they had fetched up here. Ruth's mother had seen the advertisement for a campsite caretaker, and because the day had been a fine one and they had both felt like a trip to the seaside, they had come to enquire about it. It was early summer, and the campsite was full. The hedgerows that bordered the fields were tangled with forget-me-nots and sea-pinks and poppies. Far out in the estuary yachts bobbed like butterflies in a field. 'Let's stay!' Ruth begged. Her mother smiled down at her. 'We'll try it,' she promised.

Ruth loved it at Red Rocks. She used to watch the new families as they arrived and make up names for them to share with her mother: 'Famous Five go Camping' or 'The Happy Family' or 'The Birdwatchers'. The little children shyly let her into their games. The older ones always ignored her, but she watched them lovingly. She saw romances flare and fade, and she involved herself deeply in all their precarious emotions.

Her mother was happy there, too. She enjoyed gossiping with the adults as they came to book themselves in or to buy odds and ends of food from the little store she kept in the caravan. During the winter she had found herself a part-time job at the local cinema. At Easter Ruth had left school for good. She felt as if the campsite job was hers now, especially when her mother was out at the cinema.

'Don't let me down, now,' her mother warned her, the first time she left her in charge. Ruth tidied up their caravan. She drew up a new account book, using three different coloured pens. She made sure the small washrooms were spotless, always, and when she saw new arrivals coming she was ready for them and smiling in the caravan, as though they were friends already, or come to join her family.

'Talk to the big girls,' her mother said, and Ruth made an effort to approach them, shy. But she seemed too young for them. So she chose her friends in secret and watched them. When she wasn't busy she'd squat by the tent or the caravan of her chosen friends and watch them come and go, and when they left the site she would run after their car, waving and smiling, and they, amused, sad for her, would wave back.

And now the summer had gone wrong. Over the past few weeks the visitors had left the field, weary of seeking shelter in the tiny strip of shadow cast by the tents and the caravans, defeated by the heat and by the invading crawl of ladybirds in their food and their clothes and their sleeping bags. When the last few were leaving Ruth didn't even wait in the caravan to say goodbye to them. She crouched in the rocks at the bottom of the field, hiding from them.

Ruth slept fitfully the night her mother told her they were leaving, dreaming that the field was crowded with human-sized ladybirds in tents and caravans, every inch of space taken, with more of them peering over the hedges. Rain streamed down, the colour of blood, and every drop bubbled and burst to spawn more ladybirds.

'Ruth!' her mother had to shake her awake the next morning. 'Ruth! Up! I'm going to town. Are you coming?'

'What for?'

'I'm going to find a job, and somewhere to live. We're not staying here, Ruth. I can't stand it.'

'I'm not leaving,' Ruth told her. 'I'm old enough to do as I like now.'

'You!' her mother laughed. 'You're a child!'

'Anyway, he always finds you in towns!' Ruth called after her.

Her mother hurried away from the caravan, her sandals flicking up the dry earth dust. Ruth made herself some breakfast and wandered outside with it. The day was scorching-hot already. She gathered some twigs from the hedgerows and carried them under her arms down to the bay. She lay for a long time flat on her belly on the sand, watching the ladybirds tipping and tumbling into the warm corrugations the tide had left. They fascinated her. She didn't mind them crawling on her flesh. After a time she nursed the low bed of grey charcoal back into life and toiled backwards and forwards across the hot soft sand, carrying her loads, watching out for Paul, and when she saw him coming she smiled to herself and stopped looking.

He came on to the rock and dropped a large kitchen bucket on to the sand beside her. Neither of them spoke. After a while he went over to the hedge to pull branches off, tossed them down on to the sand and jumped down after them. He watched the girl curiously. Her intent round face gave away no age at all. She was like no girl he had ever met. He knew that if he was with his friend Griffo they would laugh at her. He pictured himself sitting on the rocks with Griffo.

'What's fat and red and black all over?'

'That girl covered in ladybirds.'

'Hey,' he said. 'Why are you burning those things?'

She stared at him. 'To get rid of them.'

'But . . .' he swung his arm round in a helpless circle. 'There's millions of them!'

'Then we'll have to hurry,' she said placidly. 'They're spoiling our summer.' She jerked her head towards the campsite. 'They've all gone home now. I hate it when they all go home.'

She bent to her bucket again. She had dragged it across from the slipway, but now it was too heavy for her to lift. She glanced up at him and he laughed.

She stood back, arms akimbo, watching him. Her fat child's feet curled in the sand as she steadied herself.

The red mass in the bucket writhed languorously; reminded him of a fish cast up on land, gasping.

'I can't burn it,' he said.

Don't laugh, Griffo. Could you?

'I can't lift it,' she said.

He lifted the bucket at last, aimed, and closed his eyes. The fire hissed as the bucket grew light in his hands, and he felt his throat clenching and unclenching and his teeth grinding together. Ruth sighed. He handed her the bucket and bundled twigs hastily on to the fire.

They sat down under the rock, away from the sting of the smoke.

'Do you kiss girls?' she asked.

Paul jerked his head away from her, cancelling his smile of astonishment.

Can't answer that one, Griffo.

'Boys never kiss me.' Her voice was dull, and he risked another quick glance at her. She wasn't even looking at him. 'On our site, they're always going round kissing each other. My mum says it's indecent. She says they won't do it to me though, because I'm not like that. She says I'm witless.' She giggled suddenly, shy. 'She says I'm like those ladybirds. I'm harmless enough so long as I don't make a nuisance of myself.'

Paul held his breath.

'What's it like, kissing?' She swung her head round to look at him, lifted her hair away from her eyes, fearless.

He shrugged. 'Dunno,' he said, intent on the warm sand he was rifling through his fingers. 'Dunno.'

Help, Griffo.

She snatched up her bucket and ran off, swinging it like a small child, and dropped to her knees, her hands cupped, her face intent.

'Just half-fill it, then you can manage it on your own,' he called roughly. But if she heard him, she didn't answer.

When Paul reached the holiday flat his father told him that they were leaving the next day.

'Your mother's had enough, Paul,' he said. 'Look at her. It's drained the life out of her.'

'I'd be far better off at home,' she agreed, puffing her lips out like a fish, Paul thought. 'We'll all be better off at home.'

'Can't we just stay till the end of the week?' Paul asked. 'I mean, the weather might break by then.'

'It might,' his father agreed, surprised. 'Feels as if it's going to bust up soon, if something doesn't happen.'

'And it might not!' his mother sighed. 'What's up with you! He's been loping round the place like a trapped spider all week and now we want to go he wants to stay!'

'Just for a few days,' Paul muttered, embarrassed. He didn't understand himself. When he closed his eyes he saw ladybirds, and he saw the girl, shy, laughing at him.

'Met someone, have you?' his father suggested casually. He stretched out his newspaper like a tent.

'Sort of,' Paul muttered.

The newspaper moved. His mother raised her eyebrows.

'It's not like that.' Paul found himself blushing fiercely. He closed his eyes and the ladybirds came back, and the girl, waiting for his help, toiling backwards and forwards through the day's terrible heat. 'OK. Let's go home tomorrow. I don't mind.'

'We'll see,' his father said. 'Maybe there's something in the air, Paul. More than we know about.' He lowered his paper and winked at his son. 'Eh?'

Ruth's mother returned to the campsite during the afternoon. She went down to the bay to look for the girl but didn't see her, crouched as she was under the overhang with Paul. She could be anywhere. The woman went back to the caravan and quickly packed up her own things, checked that there was enough food for the girl to last her the rest of the week, and wrote a telephone number in the last page of the account book. Then she went, shuddering as she stepped over the crawl of red on the steps. She found a phone box near the station and phoned the same number. Her husband answered.

'Will you have Ruth back?' she asked.

Her husband was overjoyed. 'Ruthie! Of course I'll have her back. I want you both back . . .'

'Give her a few days,' his wife interrupted him. 'She'll phone you.' She put the receiver down quickly, before the break in her voice gave her away. The best thing, she told herself as she picked up her bags again.

The best the best the best.

By the time evening came the air was so still and heavy that Paul felt as if he needed to cut away chunks of it in order to move about in it. He went outside. The sky was almost green. Within seconds of leaving the house he was clammy with sweat. He no longer brushed the crawling ladybirds away from his skin. His footsteps echoed between the walls of the silent houses with a queer ringing sharpness. The peculiar bloom in the sky deepened to bruising. Seagulls flung themselves into its colour, brilliant white flecks.

He was on the sands when the first crack came. Then the rains came, huge, slow drops, sliding over him, separate beads bursting. He held up his arms and his face to it, drinking it. The sky snapped with electricity.

He thought about the girl, and he began to run, the damp sand claggy already under the soles of his shoes. His shirt was soaked; rain streamed through his hair and into his eyes. He leapt pools as he came to them, hardly breaking his stride and laughing as he splashed, roaring back at the rolling thunder; exhilarated by the energy of the storm and by the gashes of lightning that ripped the sky.

By the time he reached Red Rocks small rivers were gushing from them. He slithered across the boulders and jumped down to the black and sodden remains of the fire, and there, underneath the overhang of rock where they had talked that afternoon, lay the girl. She was curled up, asleep, with her bundle of twigs beside her.

Rain pittered down from the overhang and washed over her skin. She murmured when he shook her. 'I'm not going away. Leave me alone.'

He stood up, helpless, oblivious of the rain beating down on him.

'Let me take you home,' he said, crouching down to her.

She curled herself up away from him into the rock. Her hands were blistered, her limbs were aching. Her skin was feverish to touch.

'You can't stay here,' Paul urged.

Her mouth was dry. 'Please let me stay.'

He stood up again. He had no idea what to do. He didn't know whether she was ill with the heat or exhaustion or just pretending, playing a child's game with him. The burnt twigs slithered apart. Water from the rocks gushed into the plastic bucket, toppling it.

'You must go home. Please.'

Another brief blast of thunder seemed to kick the very rock they were sheltering under. Its violence was suddenly a terrifying, alien thing. Paul's instincts were to run from it, head down into the weather, feet slapping across the sand, and not to stop until he reached home and his parents. Instead he bent down and lifted Ruth up. Her weight fell against him as he stood up, so that he had to bend backwards slightly, his arms hooked up round her neck and the backs of her knees, his shoulder pressed forward to hold her head up. She was heavier than he'd expected. The muddy sand dragged his feet. He staggered across to the lower rocks with her, remembering the leaning caravan in the field. Perhaps someone there would help. He felt the weight of her like his own body. His feet hardly moved. His neck and his arms ached. She lay with her hair swung back and her face closed. Scared, he bent his head down and felt the warmth of her breath on his cheek. He squelched through the mud near the caravan and eased himself up the wooden steps. The door swung open, blowing an open notebook off the table.

The caravan looked deserted. It was as if no one lived here any more.

Paul tipped Ruth forward on to the narrow bunk bed, and settled the blanket round her. Rain drummed into the silence, spilling from the drowning trees on to the roof, trickling through a small hole on to the caravan floor. Paul smoothed her wet hair from her face, like a father to a child, then, leaning forward, kissed her.

6 Sweet Caroline

Caroline trailed behind her grandmother. The road was full of rubble and yellow dust. On either side diggers and bulldozers were throbbing like huge insects. Daily the honey-coloured shells of new hotels seemed to spring out of the earth.

'Gran, how can you stand this racket all the time?'

'You get used to it,' her grandmother said. 'And it can't go on for ever. Think how lovely it will be when it's finished.'

'It was probably much nicer before they started.'

Caroline thought longingly of England, with its cold, wet, wintry streets, but she kept her thoughts to herself. Her grandparents had paid for her flight over to stay with them in their winter apartment in Malta. The day after she left hospital after having her tonsils out they'd sent a telegram: 'Send Sweet Caroline. We're missing her.'

Even then she hadn't really wanted to come. But it was only for a week, and half of it had gone already. She'd be free to go back home soon.

'I'm really sorry we can't take you out today,' Gran said for the tenth time. Grandad had sprained his ankle tripping into a pot-hole. 'You'll enjoy exploring on your own, though. And the public transport here is so simple. Nothing can go wrong.'

Disorderly queues of holiday-makers chatted in the bus-terminal square. They were all on winter sun holidays. There wasn't a young person in sight. Caroline stood with her head down, hoping no one would notice her. Gran was looking at the map.

'Where would you like to go? Valletta? Rabat?'

The names meant nothing to Caroline. She stared at the row of little snub-nosed green buses. Another was just pulling up to join the line. It was gleaming with green and eggshell-blue paint. The round headlamps looked just like eyes, wide awake with surprise and fun.

'I'll go on that one.'

'Number 51.' Gran peered at her timetable. 'I don't think I know that route.'

'It's a lovely bus,' said Caroline. 'I'd really like a ride on it. I don't really care where it's going.' The bus began to rev up. Caroline ran to it. 'Bye Gran!'

It was the first time Caroline had shown any enthusiasm for

anything since she came. 'I do believe,' Gran told her husband later, 'that our little Caroline has fallen in love with a bus!'

That was the day Caroline met Victor.

When she was paying her twenty-cent fare Caroline noticed two things. First, that the driver was only a few years older than she was, and second, that there was a passenger seat at right angles to him, facing him across the narrow front of the bus. All the elderly people crowded down to the back in a giggling huddle, sharing horror stories about the state of their hotels and apartments. She'd heard it all before. A woman in matching flowery shorts and T-shirt tapped her on the arm. Caroline recognised her from Gran's apartment block. 'On your own today?' she asked Caroline. 'You can come and sit with me if you like.'

The driver nodded to the seat alongside him and Caroline sank down into it, blushing slightly. He glanced across at her. She noticed that his eyes were the colour of walnuts.

'You like Malta?' he asked her.

Caroline nodded. She hoped he would think it was sunburn that was making her face glow.

'English girl?'

She nodded again. She tried not to look at him. The floor and the ceiling of the bus were painted the same shining egg-shell blue. On the wall next to her face was a little brass fire extinguisher, gleaming like sunshine. She could see her reflection in it. Festooned around the driver's cab were colourful badges and holy pictures, and there was a glass case on a shelf above his head. It was edged with a fringe of golden tassels, and inside that was a blue-robed statue of the Virgin Mary, lit by a bulb that looked like a candle.

'You like my bus?'

'It's beautiful!' Caroline said. 'It's like a little house!' She dared to look at him at last. As he drove he flicked smiling sideways glances at her.

'You are London?'

'Sheffield.'

The driver fished in a box underneath his seat and brought out a handful of striped scarfs. He released a red and white one and draped it across the windscreen shelf.

'Sheffield United!'

She didn't tell him that she wasn't interested in football, or that her brother supported Sheffield Wednesday. She just smiled at him and felt warm.

'Your name?'

'Caroline.'

'My favourite name,' he said, instantly.

'Is it?' She was surprised. 'I'm named after a Neil Diamond song. My dad used to sing it when he was in a rock band.'

'I know it.'

And there he was, the driver of the most beautiful bus in the world, singing her song at the top of his voice. At the back of the bus a choir of white-haired, sun-flared holiday-makers sang out the chorus. Outside the window the sea was a deep, glimmering blue. The prickly-pear hedgerows glowed with flowers, and lemons like yellow moons blazed in the trees.

The journey ended in the square of a little village near a sandy bay. The holiday-makers piled out, as noisy and light-hearted as a class of children on a school trip. Caroline was the last to leave the bus.

'*Ciao*, Caroline,' the driver said.

'Chow,' she said awkwardly.

'I am Victor,' he told her, raising his hand to her as he drove away.

She watched his bus until it was out of sight. The woman in the flowery shorts and T-shirt called out to her and she followed her up a lane. She stood gazing over a wall at a heap of stones which, the woman told her, were the remains of Roman baths. 'See that square there?' the woman said. 'That's a Roman toilet. And it seats fifteen at a time! Three on each side!'

Twelve, thought Caroline, but she kept it to herself. The woman reminded her of her gran. The backs of her hands were flecked with brown freckles, and she had a gold ring on every finger. If she was in England now she'd be wearing boots and dark woolly clothes, scuttling to the shops between icy showers.

'All sitting there in their togas, having a good old gossip in the sunshine! Just imagine.'

Caroline went back down to the beach and ate the picnic lunch of salty cheese and dusty tomatoes that Gran had bought for her on the way to the bus station. She dipped her toes in the cold sea and then fell asleep, and dreamed that she had put on a blue robe and climbed into a glass box, a candle in one hand and a brass fire extinguisher in the other. She was shaken awake by the woman in the flowery shorts.

'You'd better hurry, love,' she was told. 'The last bus goes in ten minutes. Wouldn't do to miss that.'

Caroline was flustered. She had promised herself she would only go back in Victor's bus, and now she had left herself with no choice. All the holiday-makers flocked to the square, calling out to each other like seagulls. Caroline closed her eyes as she waited with them. She could hear the bus coming. She could feel the heat from it as it pulled up alongside her. When she opened her eyes she saw her bulgy reflection in the bumpers and knew that it was his bus. She took it all in: the car badges on the radiator grill, topped by a shining jaguar, and over the split windscreen the word FORD in big red letters. She snapped up every detail as if she were a camera. She would write it all in a diary when she got back to the apartment. She would borrow Gran's watercolours and paint a picture of Victor's bus.

On the journey home Caroline told Victor about her school and her tonsils operation. He told her he always wanted to go to England, to Sheffield in particular. Yes, he said, really, Sheffield was where he wanted to live.

'Why?'

'It must be a very beautiful town.'

Caroline imagined the little bus weaving in and out of the Supertram tracks along West Street. She saw all the sunny-faced passengers beaming out at city pedestrians. She saw herself in her front seat, waving at her school friends.

Victor leaned across and broke into her daydreams. 'What is your boyfriend called?'

'I haven't really got one.' She was blushing now, all round her neck and inside her ears. Victor laughed. She couldn't help joining in.

When they arrived at the depot Gran was waiting anxiously. Caroline stepped off Victor's bus without giving him a glance.

The next morning Caroline said, as casually as she could, that she wouldn't really mind exploring on her own again.

'Our Caroline is growing up,' said Gran, with an air of great secrecy.

'You could go to Popeye Village, as they call it,' Grandad suggested. 'They built a set there for the film, and you can walk round it. You'd enjoy that.'

Caroline was careful not to commit herself.

'You can get the 47 bus and it drops you off about a mile away.' Grandad scanned his bus-route map. 'Or,' yawning slightly, 'get the same number bus you caught yesterday and do a six-mile hike to it along the coast. But I shouldn't think you'd fancy that.'

'No,' said Caroline, not looking at him or at her smiling gran but at the filmy curtains of their apartment billowing out over the view of half-built hotels and rubble. 'I don't suppose I would.'

Half an hour later, and still breathless from running, she was sitting on the bus. She narrowly beat an old man to her seat. She knew Victor was pleased to see her.

'I'm going for a long walk today,' she told him. 'Right along the coast.'

'Mind they don't shoot you.' He laughed at her startled look and put out his hand towards her. 'They might think you are a beautiful dove in your white dress.'

'They don't really shoot birds, do they?'

'Of course. Or trap them if they sing.' He shrugged. 'We all do.'

She bit her lip and looked away from him. He stopped the bus sharply and pulled down the leather strap that opened his window. He leaned out, shouting something in his unfamiliar language, sharing a joke of some sort with a fruit seller on the kerbside. A few minutes later he turned back to Caroline, holding towards her a large red apple.

'You are my apple's eye,' he told her.

She carried the apple in her rucksack all day. By the time she reached Popeye Village she had blisters on both heels and the soles of her feet ached from walking on the crinkly rock path of the cliff-tops. Nobody had been shooting birds but she had found lots of shooting butts with blue cartridge shells scattered round them. She saw a man carrying half a dozen tiny cages of singing birds, and watched him laying nets for traps. She wanted to run to him and set the birds free. Had Victor really said 'we all do it'? She felt clouded and bewildered, her throat ached. 'People are different, that's all,' she tried to tell herself. 'People think differently.' After all, her father caught fish, didn't he?

She enjoyed looking round Popeye Village. She imagined Victor coming out of one of the tipsy houses with an anchor tattooed on his arm. She took some photographs to show her brother, and that gave her a wonderful idea. She asked a tourist if he would take a photograph of her with her camera. She smiled shyly at the lens. It was for Victor. She would send it to him when she got back to England. She wouldn't even have to say who it was from. He would pin it up among his badges and holy pictures for everyone to see. She was so pleased with the idea that she asked every tourist who came along to take a picture of her. She would send the very best one to Victor.

By the time she'd used up all her film she knew it was too late to walk back the way she'd come. The last bus home was at five. She followed the other tourists down the country lane to the 42 bus stop. Maybe Victor would change buses just for today. He knew where she'd gone. Maybe he would drive his number 51 round to this stop, just to pick her up.

As she waited at the bus stop she took his apple out of her rucksack, polished it lovingly, and put it back. She was never going to eat it. When it had shrivelled up to nothing she was going to plant the core in the garden, right over the spot where Ginger Tom was buried. She would gather its blossoms into an envelope and post them to Victor.

The bus that came was scruffy and dinted. Its seats were threadbare and it was driven by a young man with a shaved head. He had three noisy friends sitting behind him. He drove with his hands waving in the air and his head twisting round like an owl. He shouted abuse at pedestrians and other drivers out of his window, and hurtled up and down lanes as if he was in a racing car. Caroline clung on to the seat, her knuckles white, her stomach in her throat. She wanted to die. She wanted Victor to soar up to the bus like Superman in his blue vest, push the driver out of the window and take over the wheel. But he didn't. Behind her the elderly tourists chortled, 'He always gives us a thrill for our money, this one!'

Just as she was stepping off the bus she saw the 51 pulling away. She ran towards it, and just caught a glimpse of Victor's face.

The day bloomed again. She sang to herself as she ran back to the apartment. She would be on his bus again tomorrow.

Her grandparents were delighted to see her looking so cheerful.

'We'll spend the day together tomorrow,' they promised her. 'We'll take you to Mdina. After all, you've only got two days left.'

Two days left!

Desperately Caroline tried to find ways of spending the day on her own, but her grandparents were insistent.

'You can't possibly leave Malta without seeing Mdina,' Gran said. 'It's the ancient capital. We can go to the catacombs – think of that! And seeing as you like painting so much, we can take the watercolours and do some sketching. We'll spend the whole day there!'

Misery like a grey skin wrapped itself round Caroline.

It was the bleakest day of her life. She trudged behind her grandparents through the quiet streets of Mdina, and couldn't raise a smile or a word for them. She stood in the dimly lit passages of the catacombs and knew how Juliet had felt, alone in the cold darkness. She heard a party of schoolgirls shrieking with laughter and wondered how they could be so frivolous, so soulless. She felt edgy and strange. It was almost as if she was shedding her old skin, and there was a new self inside her urging to be let out.

It was late afternoon when they arrived back at Buggiba terminal. It was her last full day, and she hadn't seen Victor. Her grandparents had given up trying to cheer her out of her mood. Then, just as they were turning up the side-street to home, Grandad said, 'I hope you've taken a photo of those old buses for your dad.'

That new self began to soar inside her.

'What a good idea,' said Gran. 'You nip down to the buses, Caroline. We'll go back and start the dinner off.' She and Grandad held hands and walked slowly up the pitted street.

Caroline felt as if she were flying as she ran back to the terminus. She would have a photograph of her bus, with Victor at the driving wheel. No one would know. Every time she showed the picture of the little tubby bus she would see Victor again.

But the 51 wasn't there. People were all coming home from their days out, tired and sunburnt. The green buses were lining up like snug peas in a pod. She took a quick snap and turned away. A sudden toot made her jump. There was her bus, its headlamps flashing hello at her. Victor laughed down at her and pointed at her seat and without a second thought she stepped on to the bus and sat beside him. He had one more run to do, he told her. He had missed her.

They hurtled along the coast road, and she spilled out for him all the events of the day. All of a sudden it had been a day of delights. They laughed and joked as passengers clambered on and clambered off at their stops. Every now and then he sang snatches of her song. She leaned back and looked along the length of the bus. It was as familiar to her now as the apartment room. She would never forget how the red cables threaded their way across the eggshell-blue ceiling to the brass bell near the cab. She loved the way they made it chime. She loved the posters of gaily painted fishing boats and domed churches and knights' towers. She imagined living in the bus, polishing the fire extinguisher and the bell, scrubbing the painted floor to keep it spick and span. It would make a wonderful home. She and Victor would drive round in it to the end of their days.

If her grandparents noticed how her eyes were sparkling when she came back, or wondered how it could have taken her an hour and a half to take a photograph, they said nothing. But she couldn't sleep that night. Tomorrow evening she would be flying home again. When she had told Victor this she had promised to ride on his bus again the next morning. It would be very special. Maybe he would abandon his route and drive her round and round the island. She wouldn't mind if she missed her plane.

To Caroline's utter misery her grandparents decided to have a run on the bus with her. She didn't even look at Victor when they climbed on. They squashed up next to her in the long seat alongside Victor and chatted to him about the local racecourse. Caroline said nothing at all. She kept her head down and her hands clasped across her rucksack. She could feel the apple inside it.

They got off at a place called Mosta. They wanted to show her the church. Caroline hated churches. She hated her grandparents. She turned quickly round to Victor as they climbed off the bus ahead of her. 'I may never see you again,' she blurted out.

He leaned across, took her hand, and kissed it. 'Come back to Malta.'

'I will!' She could come back at Easter. She could spend the whole of the summer there. When she was old enough to leave home she would live there.

'*Ciao*, Sweet Caroline.'

'Chow, Victor.'

And when she jumped off the bus her gran put her arms round her shoulders and gave her a little squeeze, just as she used to do when she was about six years old and hopelessly unhappy about something. 'How about a cup of hot chocolate and a date slice?' she suggested.

When her bags were packed and she was waiting for the taxi to take her to the airport her grandad said, 'I hope you've enjoyed your little holiday, Caroline. It's no big deal really, being stuck with a couple of old fogies like us.'

Gran smiled at her.

'I've had a wonderful time!' said Caroline. 'It's the best holiday I've ever had in my whole life!'

She stepped into the taxi with a light heart. As soon as she lost sight of her grandparents' waving hands she opened her rucksack and took out the apple. She blew on it softly, her lips almost touching it. She breathed in its sweet, delicate scent.

She couldn't believe it when she saw the bus coming towards her. For a wild moment she imagined that Victor was about to hold up the taxi and kidnap her. She craned forward to wave to him. But the number 51 sailed on past her taxi, and Victor didn't even see her. He was too busy looking at the girl who was sitting beside him on Caroline's seat. They were both laughing out loud. Across the dashboard was draped a black and white scarf. The 51 bus roared past and away, away in a drizzle of yellow dust, away and out of sight, like a dream.

It was not until the taxi driver opened the door at the airport that Caroline realised she had eaten the apple. She paid the driver, walked into the departure lounge, and threw the core into the bin.

7 Hurry Please

June, and a perfect day for this visit, which I had promised myself for many years. I had a childish sense of excitement as I drove towards his cottage, through the lovely countryside of Dorset. My route took me past the church that I'd heard so much about, and on a whim I decided to stop there on my way. The day was blue and bright and welcoming as I parked my car just outside the church. Away on either side of me rolled farmed fields. House martins stitched their route above the churchyard, criss-crossing the sky with their familiar twitching flight, glancing against the walls of the church and away again as if they could never for a moment take rest there. And there were the family graves, all in a line.

It was just as I was looking at them, reading the inscriptions and pondering on the fact that so many of the males of the family bore his name, that I heard a burst of fine, lively music coming from the church. I went to the door and could hear clearly the sound of a violin and a cello, and the sweet, rough singing of country voices. I opened the door slowly, not wanting to intrude on a service but eager to hear the music more clearly. The sounds stopped at once. I pushed open the door fully and went in. There was no one there. Yet there was an echo of the music that lingered still, as though the singers and musicians had only paused, and were waiting for me to leave. I crept round the listening silence of the church and went out again, glad of the warm embrace of sunlight. I closed the door behind me and waited, half-expecting the music to start up, but there was nothing. Yet I was certain I had heard it earlier.

I wanted to take the time, even then, to stroll around the churchyard and look again at the family graves, but something was tugging me away from them. The music had certainly disturbed me, but there was more than that. I had the nagging feeling that something important had been left undone. I couldn't relax there. For a moment, as I stood hesitating in the church porch, it seemed to me that the far horizon was breaking up. Instead of the fields of neat farmland that I had seen before stretching away into the distance there seemed to be a vast dull wilderness. I could hear his words describing it – heathy, furzy, briary. Yet as soon as I came out of the churchyard I realized I was mistaken. The sun had slipped behind the clouds and dulled the light, that was all.

I returned to my car and set off on the last part of the journey, to the cottage. I parked my car and walked half a mile or so along a woodland path. Even though I had lost the full sun now I was sticky with heat. Patches of sunlight dappled through the leaves and lit clumps of bluebells and around them flies lumbered, heavy with noise. A strange feeling of urgency hurried me on. Of course I was anxious to arrive.

And at last, there it was, after so many turns and twistings. I saw first the great beech tree at the back of the cottage. I had seen pictures of it so many times that I could have drawn the cottage from memory, with its long thatched roof arching over the latticed windows, and its three tall chimneys. I hurried round to the front. No, this surely was the wrong place. Here were two buildings, leaning against each other, but separate dwellings, surely. They were very clearly a main cottage with roses and honeysuckle clinging on to its walls and spilling their perfume, and a sort of lean-to that seemed to have been tacked on to the side, with its own doorway. I stepped back a moment to look at the sign but was reassured that I had indeed come to the right place.

There came then a drumming of hooves on the lane behind me, of a horse and cart being driven with great urgency. It pulled up so close to me that I was knocked into the hedge. A man in a long-coated black suit jumped down from the cart and reached up for a black bag. He hurried past me without acknowledging my surprised greeting, down the path and into the cottage through the main door. Almost immediately the door of the smaller cottage opened and a white-haired women came out. She too was dressed in black, in the long skirts of the last century. She followed the man quickly into the main cottage.

I stood at the gate, confused and curious. Perhaps it was some sort of play, specially devised for the visitors. In that case I had arrived just in time. I heard someone coming up behind me.

'Would you hurry please?' a woman's voice said. I turned, and saw no one. 'Hurry.' I looked the other way, and distinctly felt a movement of air as if someone was brushing past me. I stepped back, then heard the click of the gate behind me. A faint sweat of fear came over me, yet still there was that nagging sense of urgency and purpose. I opened the gate and closed it, tried it again, and it gave exactly that sound I had heard. Someone had come through it. Very gently, I closed it again, and turned to the cottage. There in front of me was the cottage I had always imagined; a long single building with a path winding its way through a garden of lupins and lavender and pansies to the one front door. There was no sign now of the coach and horse, of the hurrying people. I had imagined everything.

I had come there intending to linger first in the garden and then to wander around his cottage, taking my time to explore the rooms. Now all I wanted was to turn away and go back through the woods and drive home. Perhaps I would return another time, maybe with a friend. Yet I had travelled so far to be here. I had even made an appointment to come. It didn't matter. I could come another time, I told myself. I paused with my hand on the gate. The woman's voice I had just heard echoed in my head. 'Would you hurry please.' I had heard it, and the click of the gate, the scuff of her boots on the path. I had not seen that person, but she had seen me. I had not imagined it. I had to go in.

I was greeted at the door, as if I had been expected, and was invited to walk straight into the parlour to the left of the porch.

'You've had a lot of visitors this morning,' I said lightly.

'Not at all. You're the first to come today,' I was told.

'And the play?' I felt foolish saying it. 'Has it started?'

'What play do you mean?' The warden shook his head and smiled.

I went through to the parlour feeling more than a little anxious. Yet the room was peaceful and calm. It smelled of polish, and had the quiet and ordered appearance that rooms have when they have not been lived in for a great deal of time. It was a show room. I glanced casually round, recognising the room from descriptions I had read, the floor 'footworn and hollowed and thin', the one long beam bisecting the low ceiling, and the deep inglenook, long empty of wood ash. I crossed over to the second of the two windows. I could almost hear his voice then, chanting in my head:

'Here was the former door, where the dead feet walked in.'

I tried to shake the words away. He had come from a family of builders – all kinds of changes would have been made to the cottage. At the far end of the room was a thin adzed door leading, as I knew, to his father's office, and through there to the stairs. I was unwilling to go that way yet. I felt I wanted to be out in the sunlight. I was cold. I touched the glass of the window where the flowers pressed against it and there it came again, as clear as it had been in the garden outside, the commotion of hurrying feet, the scuff of boots on stone. I felt the cool sensation of someone brushing past me, and heard again the words, 'Would you hurry please,' and knew that they were being spoken to me. But the room was empty, the only sound was the birdsong in the garden outside. I called out, 'Who's there?' The cottage was in silence. And yet now at the same time it was full of sound and movement, of panic even. I ran through to the porch, shouting, 'Didn't you see someone then, a woman? Did you let her in?' The porch was deserted.

I was just at the point of running through into the garden when I heard the sound of a woman crying out in pain from one of the upstairs rooms. The sound echoed round the cottage, rolling from room to room. Frightened though I was it was my instinct to turn back to the porch and to run right through the parlour and up the stairs. I went straight into the main bedroom of the cottage. This, I was sure, was where the cry had come from. There was not a soul to be seen there. I was about to go through to the further room when I heard a sharp intake of breath, a gasp here, a sigh from the other side – all around me, it seemed, unseen people were breathing. Then the sounds quietened down.

I steadied myself, and made myself take the time to look around me. The room was light, having windows at each side, but cool because of the low thatch which kept most of the sunlight out. The floorboards were of fine old chestnut, and most of the room was taken up by a large bed. There was certainly nobody in the room.

As I crossed over to go to the next room the gasping started again. I pressed my hands against my eyes, wishing myself well and sane again, heard footsteps on the stairs, and looked round. I had not been aware before that there was a fire lit in the grate, setting the room moving with the flickering dance of flame and shadow. Surely I would have noticed that, and been grateful for its heat. Someone was pushing past me, breathless, as if they were carrying an awkward burden. I heard the slop of water, and saw then in the firelight's shadows, half in and half out of real light, the old white-haired woman setting down a large and steaming bowl by the bed.

Now other shapes came dimly into view. They were fragmented and unfocussed, shapes and shadows first, and then they began to take form and a degree of colour. There were several people in the room. A young man was over by one of the windows, substantially blocking out the light. He had his back to the room. The older man who had arrived in the coach was stooping over the bed. He was in his shirt sleeves, and his long coat was hanging by a nail on the back of the door. By his pose I could imagine that he was a doctor. In the bed was a young woman. She was pale, lying back as if she was exhausted. A mob-capped nurse on the other side of the bed leaned across and wiped her face with a cloth. The young woman gave another gasp of pain, and I turned away towards the other window, to the reassurance of sunlight cutting out a small gold square on the floorboards. Musical instruments were leaning against the wall, a violin and a cello, put down as if carelessly, in a moment of anxiety. I wanted to touch them, to make sure for myself that they were real. Without realising it I was walking on tiptoe. I hardly dared to breathe.

As I moved I put my hand out carefully to touch the bed, to touch the figures there, to touch the instruments. There was nothing. Slowly I paced the circumference of the room, frightened almost of displacing the air with my movement. Where the figures had been there was nothing.

I felt an overwhelming sense of dread and loss, and into that sensation came the voice which I had no doubt belonged to the doctor.

'It's a boy,' he said quietly. 'But I'm afraid, Jemima, he is dead.'

He lifted up the pale, still body of a baby and, rolling it in a sheet, put it aside on a chair and bent to attend to the woman again. The man at the window, surely the husband, gave a gasp of dismay and came to the bed. It was evident to me that it was too painful for him to look at the baby. He sat down on the edge of the bed and took the young woman's hands in his own, murmuring out soft words of comfort to her. The older woman, his mother maybe, sighed and crossed herself. The doctor poured water from the jug at the washstand and soaped his hands. He was distressed. He had done his job as well as he could.

'I'll leave you to the monthly nurse and to your family,' he said. 'I have more work to do in the village.'

Those moments seemed to last for ever. There was nothing to be done, nothing anyone could do, it seemed. The family quietened into a sad, exhausted resignation. Yet now over their silence I could hear the sound of other voices, rising and falling in echo, clamouring for attention. They seemed to be coming from every corner of the room, from the fields outside, from the air itself – I felt I could drown in the welter of sounds, the voices of men and women and children, soldiers and farmers and country girls, marching and dancing and calling out, their words jostling like the insistent buzzing of summer insects in a garden. Every now and again I caught something familiar in the words they were saying, as if I had heard them spoken before, as if they were shouting to me out of my memory. I was washed in their sea of sadness and panic. And clearly through all the sounds came that first voice again, at my side this time, a woman's voice speaking to me: 'Would you hurry please?'

None of the family in the room had looked at the dead baby on the chair. I crouched down to it, anxious to catch a glimpse of what might have been. I knew exactly who it was. I was sure then that I saw just the tiniest movement of his fingers. It was as if a butterfly had moved tiny wings. Surely he was alive.

There it came again. It was the slightest flexing of a finger. I put my cheek to his lips, and felt the smallest kiss of air. He was alive.

'He's not dead!' I shouted. 'Listen to me. He's not dead!'

But there was no way of making them hear me. The doctor rolled down his sleeves, the nurse held out his coat for him. The old mother stooped to pick up the bowl and carry it away. The husband drew close the curtains so his young wife could sleep.

'He's not dead!' I shouted into their faces, but there was nothing I could do to make them listen to me. I tried to lift up the child but my hands slipped through empty air. And still the voices clamoured round me, begging for attention.

'He's not dead!' I shouted again. Frantic now, I looked round for some way of attracting the attention of the figures in the room. I felt in my pockets and found there the book that I had brought, and that I had been reading again the night before. Instinctively I flung it on the floor in front of the nurse, just as she was handing the doctor his bag. As if something had startled her, she looked towards the direction of the sound. There was no book there for her to see. She heard the sound from somewhere in her imagination, I think.

Slowly she put down the bag and reached over to where the baby was bundled up in its shawl. With one hand to her mouth she moved away a corner of the sheet. The baby's fist unclenched.

'Dead!' she cried. 'Stop a minute! He's alive enough, sure!'

I leaned back against the wall, faint with exhaustion. The voices drizzled around me, too fragmented now to catch. I saw the doctor and the nurse attending to the child, heard at last his first strong cry, saw him being lifted into the air and put into his young mother's arms.

'Thomas,' her husband said. 'Young Thomas Hardy is born.'

In the way that the shadows of moving shapes are cast by firelight around a room and then extinguished, so the figures in the room dissolved. A great peace descended on the cottage, and on me. I believe I went into a kind of deep sleep there, standing as I was. Certainly I was startled into wakefulness by the sound of a sudden burst of laughter coming from outside. I looked out of the window, into the dazzle of sun, and saw that the garden was full of people, visitors like myself, taking photographs, crouching to smell the flowers. Soon the cottage would be invaded by them. Already now I could hear voices in the room below me. I went through the narrow doorway and heard footsteps behind me.

'Just a moment,' a young woman said.

I knew her voice.

I turned, and she came softly towards me, holding out a book. 'I think you dropped this.'

I took it from her. '*Tess of the D'Urbervilles*,' I said. 'I would hate to lose this. Thank you.'

'Not at all,' she said, and turned to go away. 'Thank you.'

8 Nightmare

Rab lives over the railway lines, near the allotments. He doesn't always live there; sometimes I don't see him for weeks or even months, and then he just turns up again as if he's never been away. He lives in an old shed that needs pulling down – it's more of a barn really, with high heavy doors. He says it's all that's left of his estate, that long ago his family lived in a big house that was bombed in the war, and that all the allotments are really on his land. His granddad's a horse-dealer; they go round the country together to horse fairs and markets. I don't think Rab gets to school much; he's supposed to go to the one by the allotments when they're here, but I don't think he's got a lot of time for that sort of learning. They're a bit like gypsies, really. I'm not supposed to have anything to do with him, but I do. I can't help it. If you knew Rab you'd understand.

He hangs round and waits for me to come over the hill from school, and I see him leaning against the big chestnut tree or sitting astride the wall near our house and I think, 'Great! Rab's back!'

I wish he hadn't come this winter though.

'Coming on moors?' he asks me, as if I only saw him yesterday. 'Coming up to Downpour?' And before I know it I've run in to change into old clothes that I'm allowed to get mucky, and I'm racing over the moors with him, scrambling over those massive boulders that he says are fossilised dinosaur droppings, and slithering behind the waterfall to the dark cave behind it that we call the Downpour Den. 'Cavemen lived here,' he tells me, and his voice bounces round the dripping hollows. 'You're standing on the dust of their bones.' I know it's true. 'We'd be all right here, if there was a Big Bang. We could come here and live.'

Rab isn't a house person. He isn't much older than me, but he knows everything. I'm sure that's because he isn't a house person. He lives in the hut with his granddad, Ged, who's a grimy-looking cold and sour fellow; he never speaks to me; I'm not sure I like him at all. And when they feel like going they just go. I hate it. I never know they've gone. I go down to their hut and try to peer in through the one high window, but they have stringy curtains draped across and there's nothing to see in there. There's a smell of Rab and Ged though, whether they're there or not. People have tried to get that hut knocked down while they're away, but they can't. It belongs to Rab and his granddad. It's their home.

'I wish you wouldn't go without telling me,' I say to him. 'I hate that, not saying goodbye and that.'

That always makes him laugh. 'What's the point of saying goodbye?' he says. 'I know I'll be coming back.'

Last time Rab turned up was in the dead of last winter. I wish I hadn't seen him. It was after Christmas, and I was just going up our road to the post and there he was, hunched up in the cold by the chestnut tree. The snow had come a few days before and now it was packed ice.

It was an effort to walk upright.

'All right, Rab?' I shouted, pleased to see him, but not showing it.

'Coming up to Downpour?' he asked me.

'Eh, it's freezing!' I said. 'We'll never get over moors in this lot.'

'Get your boots on,' he told me, not even looking at me, holding his white hands up to his mouth as though he was trying to melt his fingers with his breath. 'See you at moorgates. There's something I want to tell you.'

I always do what Rab says. I can't help it. Half an hour later I'd got my thickest clothes on and my boots and I was standing by the white stile that leads off up to the open moorland, stamping on a patch of ice that was iron-hard. Nothing moved. The sun was lemon-yellow but there was no heat from it at all, and all the blades of grass and bells of dead heather were clamped in their own ice-shells.

I heard Rab whistle, and I saw him come out onto the footpath about a quarter of a mile on from where I was standing. I waved and swung myself over the stile, lost my footing on the last slippery step and sprawled head first into the ice-blades. By the time I'd picked myself up Rab was out of sight, but I knew the way off by heart and slithered after him, my heart jerking into my throat every time I lost my footing. I caught up with him at the Edge. He was sitting with his legs dangling over a drop of nearly a hundred foot, looking out across the deep white floor of the valley. I eased myself onto the slab next to him. In summer you can hear the curlews up here, and the cackling of the grouse on the moors, and the sheep yelling to each other across the slopes, but today, when my panting had died down, there was nothing. Not a sound.

'Everything's died,' I said.

'The winter solstice,' Rab said. 'Everything's standing still. The sun, and the grass, and the streams, and the birds. Nothing moving.'

'You'd think it was waiting for something.'

'There's nothing to wait for now. It's too late.'

You don't expect Rab to sound like that, with that kind of sadness in his voice. He pulled himself up and spat over the Edge. We listened out for the tiny splat as it struck rock, and laughed. That was more like it.

'Gozzing's good for you,' he told me. 'Clears your passages. If you swallow your gozz it clogs up all your works.'

He set off carefully over a boulder that was completely cased in ice, and then started running, his boots striking the iron of the ground like flints, a kind of urgency; I lost sight of him as he ran and could only hear the chime of his stride, and then I heard nothing but my own steps as I stumbled and slid, and the rapid rasp of my breath. I skidded at last down the slope to the Downpour, and brought myself to a halt against the squat stone we called toad-rock. From here the narrow track twists round and comes below the cascading force of the waterfall. Because of the twist of the valley you don't hear anything from this side of toad-rock. As soon as you scramble round it to the jut of the path you're deafened by its clamour; it drowns out everything, and the spray from it showers over you – no escaping till you ease yourself behind it into the den.

I edged myself round the glassy rock-foot, and then I was struck by the weight of silence. The whole waterfall was frozen – I could see great limbs of icicles sprouting from the overhang, and the green-white sheen of a huge slab of ice draped across the mouth of Downpour Den, like a curtain. The silence was heavier than the noise I'd expected – it was like a pressure waiting to burst, waiting to explode into splinters and tumble down the boulder scree to the valley.

Rab was clinging onto a rock near the overhang, and I made my way over to him, hugging the slippery skin of the stones with both hands as I went; but when I reached him and looked up at last into the frozen curtain that hung over the Downpour I saw something that was so terrifying that I'll never get it out of my mind, that I think of every day, as if it's part of me now. It was this: a horse, trapped in the ice; a great black horse, its legs straddled so its hooves were planted firmly in bed-rock, its head lifted, teeth bared in fright, its eyes staring; locked in death.

I think I crawled back up on my hands and knees till I was on ground where I felt safe enough to stand, and then I started running, feet splaying out each side of me, my head pounding and dizzy; when I couldn't breathe any more I turned round to wait for Rab, but he was nowhere in sight. I could have sworn I'd heard him scrabbling back up the slope after me, and the thud of his boots on the hard rocks. I waited a bit but the cold began to seep into me; I couldn't stop myself from shaking, still in shock from the sight of the horse frozen into its glassy tomb. Besides, Rab knew many routes over the moors – he could be anywhere. I jogged back home, glad of the comforting warmth of our house, and the quiet normal talking of my mum and dad in the kitchen.

I couldn't sleep that night. Mum had gone to bed early and Dad was playing his jazz in the front room. Usually I love to listen to music when I'm in bed; in the end it always drowses me off to sleep. I went downstairs and got myself a drink, then wandered into the back room. We don't use that room much in winter; it's a cold room, because we're on the edge of town and the wind comes off the moors onto the back of the house, and we made the mistake of putting big sliding door-windows in to give us a better view. I went over to the window now. The curtain had been pulled across to keep out the draught, but I thought I'd like to look at the moors in the moonlight, the blue-white gleam of the snow. Just before I reached the window I heard Rab's voice, calling my name very softly from outside. It was almost as if I'd known he'd be there.

I tugged at the curtain with one hand, sipping at my hot chocolate, and there instead of the sliding window was a huge slab of ice, and frozen into it, the black horse.

Its eyes were wide open and its ears pressed back, and its yellow teeth were bared in fright. As I watched in the same lock of fear it reared back its head. In slow motion its front legs carved an upwards arc and flung black hooves to pound against the ice; I could hear the sweet breathy sound of the saxophone in the other room, and I could hear the pounding of the hooves, and ice tearing in front of me, above and around me, the splintering and crinkling as a thousand tiny bright shards showered over me, sharp as glass, bright as water. Hooves flailed as the black horse reared again, with hot life snorting from his nostrils. And clinging on to his back, laughing down at me, was Rab.

'Come on!' he shouted. 'Up on moors.' He leaned down, one arm tucked into the horse's mane, and heaved me up in front of him.

I can feel the way my legs ached as they stretched across the black sinewy back, and the lurching sensation beneath me as we galloped over the moors. I'd never ridden a horse in my life, and I was jolted from side to side and up and down with the unfamiliar movement. Rab had his arm round my waist to stop me from slipping off, and I remember the ice-cold pressure of his fingers. I dug my fingers into the mane and clung onto it; it felt like thick, silky hair. The air on my cheeks was raw, and as we plunged into the black bitter night, away from the houses, away from the lights, I felt as if all my known world was slipping away from me; and that this was where I'd rather be, riding forever in cold air. We soared over the white stile of moorgates and thundered up the familiar whitened tracks, with the stars hanging and turning like icicles. Gleaming boulders loomed up and away from us. We were streaming fast, floating; we were in a different element, like water.

I recognised the squat bulk of the toad-rock, where the scree slope fell away from us; I recognised the splintered ice-curtain of the Downpour, and as the horse leapt across the mouth of it into the black cavern behind I tried to slide off his back . . .

'No!' I screamed. 'Not there!'

Rab laughed, his ice-cold hands pressing into my ribs, and his laugh echoed and bounced in the hollows of the caves. 'Stay with me,' he urged. 'Don't leave me.'

I heard a creaking above my head, and watched the slow

languorous curtain of ice slide down to envelop the cave, felt the intense chill of it as it scraped across my skin, trapping me . . .

My dad found me standing in the dark in the back room. He took the cup of cold chocolate out of my hand.

'You've had a nightmare,' he said. 'You're all right.'

I jerked back the curtain, expecting to find the window shattered, and the snow on the lawn outside swirled round with the kicking of hooves, but there was nothing to see, only the moors cold and quiet in the moonlight, and the stars, like twisting icicles.

'There was a horse,' I told Dad. 'It carried me off to the Downpour . . .'

He led me back upstairs to my room. 'People used to think,' he told me, 'that wild horses came in the night and carried them off to terrible places. That's why it's called a nightmare. Go to sleep now. You'll be all right.'

But I had no intentions of sleeping ever again. I sat bolt upright in my bed with the light on, listening out for the stamp of hooves on the iron earth, and for Rab.

The next day was the beginning of the new term. It stayed just below freezing all day, but the sun was bright and the sky was a kind of fierce blue. It was the sort of day that Rab and I liked to go up on the moors, when you could see for miles from the Edge, all the little villages and roads in the valley, and the river winding slowly through. I couldn't get Rab off my mind that day. I wanted to tell him about my dream. I wondered if he'd had the same one. We'd tried to do that many times – we'd told each other that we would try to dream the same thing, and meet up in our dreams. We'd nearly done it once – we'd both dreamt of the Downpour Den one night, but there'd been no people in either of our dreams. Why had he laughed, in my dream? Why had he wanted to be trapped in the ice-cave, when I'd been so frightened? And even as I thought of all these things that I wanted to ask him about, the idea came to me just as powerfully as it had done last night, that it hadn't been a dream at all, but that it had really happened.

And there was another thing that bothered me. When we'd gone up to the Downpour yesterday he'd said there was something he wanted to tell me. He'd taken me to see the horse, but he hadn't told me anything, except that it was the winter solstice. I knew that. I knew that we'd had midwinter's night before Christmas, and that it was as if nothing grew around that time, waiting for the sun to move near our part of the earth again. '*It's too late.*' That was what he'd said.

I had to stay behind after school to help get all last term's art work down from the walls, and by the time I left it was nearly dark. I hurried down to the allotments. It was bitterly cold down there, directly exposed to the moors, and there was very little light left.

The town lights were behind me. I picked my way along the path. A stray cat yowled at me from its ratting place near the whitened mound of the compost heap. I found my way by memory to the high bulk of Rab's shed, and I could tell that it was in darkness.

I went up to it all the same, and tried to peer in through that high curtained window. Surely they hadn't gone again so soon? I was just about to move away when I heard a movement inside; a kind of hollow knocking. 'Rab?' I shouted. 'You in there?' There was silence, but then the knocking came again; but it wasn't knocking at all, it was stamping, and I knew the sound from the farmers' yards down in the valley. It was the impatient clopping sound of a horse's hooves. I backed away, and the stamping began again, more urgent this time. The high wooden door of the hut shook, and I knew that the horse inside was rearing up against it, beating its hooves, trying to tear it down.

'Stop it!' I shouted, hardly realising what I was doing. 'I know what you are. You're not a horse at all. You're only a nightmare.'

I started to run, skidding on the slippery path as I went. But how could it be a nightmare, when the lights of my town were blinking like low yellow stars in front of me, and I could hear the drone of cars making for the motorway? Behind me was the thundering of hooves pounding on wood, and the terrible splintering as the door began to give way.

I ran wildly towards the warm familiar town lights, and as the path turned to stubbed grass and then met the pavement I skidded on the ice, fell headlong and closed my eyes, wanting to sleep . . .

'All right, love? Come on. Up you get. No bones broken.'

Davey Brown, an old friend of my dad's, hauled me up and brushed me down.

'You're shaking like a plate of jelly. Come on, get in my car, and I'll run you home. I want a word with your dad anyway, about the new allotment hut . . . In you get.'

I was glad of his offer. Davey had left the engine running when he stopped to help me up, and the car was still warm.

'Good job I saw you fall,' he said, as we pulled away into the traffic. 'You must have been going at quite a pace to come down like that. Shouldn't run on ice, you know.'

'I saw a horse,' I said. 'It scared me.'

'A horse?'

'I didn't exactly see it,' I added. 'I heard it. On the allotments.'

He shook his head. 'I doubt it. How would a horse get there? Whereabouts on the allotments?'

It felt safer now, in the warmth of the car. It was comforting to be told that I must have imagined it. I didn't mind if he laughed at me. I wanted to be brought away from the nightmare.

'I thought I heard it,' I said, 'in the hut.'

'But there isn't a hut,' Davey said. 'Not any more.'

Not any more. I began to shiver violently again now. Nightmare and reality became one thing, as I walked again in my memory down the dark track, past the cat crouching in the hedge, saw the looming shape of the hut, peered through the window, touched the wood of the door . . .

'We pulled it down over the weekend,' Davey went on. 'Real eyesore, that thing. That's why I'm wanting a word with your dad about building us a dry, secure little hut for the allotment users to keep their tools and seeds and things in. We've been wanting one on that site for years . . .'

We waited for the traffic lights to change. Was I really in Davey's car, I wondered, or was I still lying on the ice, or peering through the hut window, or chasing Rab over the moors, or looking at the frozen slab, of the Downpour . . .

'But it's their home,' I managed to say, trying to get him to talk again. As long as Davey talked, surely I was in the car next to him, safe and warm, and on my way home. 'They live there.'

'Old Ged? He came up a few days ago. He wanted to collect a few bits and pieces that he'd left behind. But he'll not be coming back, he said. Not without the lad. I expect your mum and dad told you, didn't they? Terrible business, that.'

We had arrived at our house. I followed him down the jennel and into the kitchen. Mum sat me down by the radiator and gave me a hot drink and got on with preparing the meal while my dad and Davey worked out a price agreement for the hut they were wanting on the allotments. I went out into the back room while they were talking, and I drew back the heavy curtains and looked out across the dark plain of the moors. Something outside was dripping, very slowly, very softly.

My mother came in and stood beside me.

'Shall I tell you about Rab?' she said.

Dread slowed the thumping of my blood.

'Listen,' I said. 'It's thawing.'

'Yes. The forecast said temperatures would go up tonight.' She touched my arm. 'I thought you and Rab had stopped seeing each other years ago. That's why I didn't tell you.'

'Rab was my best friend,' I said.

I didn't look at her while she was telling me. I didn't listen to her. I knew already what had happened to him. I listened instead to Rab and myself talking quietly together, sitting next to each other on the Edge, the day he showed me the frozen horse.

'*Everything's died.*'

'*The winter solstice. Everything's standing still. The sun, and the grass, and the streams, and the birds. Nothing moving.*'

'*You'd think it was waiting for something.*'

'*There's nothing to wait for now. It's too late.*'

'Rab was killed about three weeks ago,' my mother was saying. 'He stole a ride on somebody's horse, and it took fright and threw him. He died on midwinter's day. The longest night of the year.'

The dripping from the roof had turned into a trickle. I could see it coursing down the outside of the window; ice running free again. Tomorrow the Downpour would crack and burst and gush back to life. But I would never see Rab again. I thought of him, a free spirit, urging the black horse on over the moors, riding free, laughing.

BERLIE DOHERTY

Granny was a Buffer Girl

Winner of the Carnegie Medal.

Leaving home . . .

It's hard for Jess to imagine what it will be like, separated from her family and friends and the place she has always known. As her departure approaches, it is time for her to share in the family secrets – the love stories, and the ghost stories . . .

There's Bridie and Jack, whose love was strong enough to keep them together despite the divisions between their families. Dorothy, for whom the admiration of a rich young man seems to offer an escape from the toil and dirt of her job buffing up cutlery. Then, of course, there's Jess's own story. She, too, has known moments of both grief and happiness.

BERLIE DOHERTY

White Peak Farm

The story of a close-knit family living in an isolated community. The changes which the family have to face, and which Jeannie, the teenage daughter, herself experiences when she falls in love for the first time, are superbly described by this skilled storyteller, winner of the Carnegie Medal for *Dear Nobody* and *Granny Was a Buffer Girl*.

'an engrossing novel . . .'
Valerie Bierman, *Scotsman*

'a sensitive and perceptive story . . . Its strength lies in the author's understanding and vivid portrayal of the individual members of the family . . . warmth, humanity and deep understanding of the real values of life.'
British Book News

'carefully observed and neatly crafted . . .'
Times Educational Suplement

EDITED BY MIRIAM HODGSON

In Between

First kisses, standing up for other people and making decisions on one's own. Eleven funny, sad and brave stories about growing-up, reflecting the moment when childhood is left behind.

The prize-winning and best-selling contributors are: Vivien Alcock, Rachel Anderson, Joanna Carey, Adèle Geras, Elizabeth Laird, Sam McBratney, Michael Morpurgo, Alick Rowe, Ian Strachan, Robert Westall and Jacqueline Wilson.

'An excellent collection . . . A must . . .'
School Librarian

'strong, involving stories.'
Junior Bookshelf

'A strong and interesting collection . . .'
Books for Keeps